And she echoed his need, feeling the hard male outline of his body imprinted on her soft flesh. His roaming hands were impatient with the restrictions of her interfering clothes, and Annette felt a similar frustration.

"This isn't enough for you, either, is it?" Josh demanded thickly.

A faint shudder went through her as he framed her face with his hands. His breathing was raggedly disturbed, and desire smoldered in his eyes. Annette gazed at him with raw wonder, shaken by her own desires.

"Let's go to my suite." His suggestion fell somewhere between a request and a command, insisting while offering her a choice.

She murmured her agreement, vaguely stunned that she could sound so calm when she'd just made such a momentous decision.

JANET DAILEY AMERICANA

Janet Dailey
Americana

THAT CAROLINA SUMMER

Harlequin Books

TORONTO • NEW YORK • LONDON
AMSTERDAM • PARIS • SYDNEY • HAMBURG
STOCKHOLM • ATHENS • TOKYO • MILAN
MADRID • WARSAW • BUDAPEST • AUCKLAND

The state flower depicted on the cover of this book is
dogwood.

Janet Dailey Americana edition published October 1987
Second printing September 1988
Third printing September 1989
Fourth printing September 1990
Fifth printing November 1991

ISBN 0-373-21933-4

Harlequin Presents edition published March 1982

Original hardcover edition published in 1982
by Mills & Boon Limited

THAT CAROLINA SUMMER

CHAPTER ONE

THE LANGUID HEAT of the North Carolina sun was mildly enervating, countered by a soft breeze off the Atlantic Ocean. Bending a knee, Annette Long smoothed the tanning oil over her palely golden leg. Her smoky gray gaze idly circled the large swimming-pool area, taking note of the other guests enjoying the resort's facilities.

A young couple splashed in the pool, shrieking their laughter as they tried dunking each other, but most others lazed in the lounge chairs provided by the hotel, involving themselves in activities no more strenuous than applying suntan lotion to their bodies, as Annette was doing.

Finishing, she capped the bottle and turned to her sister. A faint smile touched her mouth, affectionate yet bemused. There was dark-haired, blue-eyed Marsha with a book in hand and dressed in a conservative one-piece blue swimsuit. At eighteen Marsha had everything it took to be a very attractive woman, but she was so quiet and unassuming she didn't make use of her assets, resisting Annette's attempts to take her in hand.

Sometimes it was difficult for Annette to believe they were sisters, the contrast between them was so sharp. Annette simply didn't possess her younger sister's retiring personality. In fact, she was the complete opposite, boldly confident and aggressive enough to go after what she wanted. Their physical appearance differed, as well. Annette's shoulder-length hair was the tawny blonde of sherry, styled in soft feather curls as opposed to the rather severe boyish cut of Marsha's brunette hair, which did nothing to enhance her natural looks. Marsha's eyes were a sky blue and Annette's were smoke colored with the fire of a keen intelligence glittering in them.

Both sisters were slim and a little above average height, but while Marsha concealed her nicely shaped figure in conservative outfits, Annette showed hers off. Her white swimsuit was one-piece, too, but it certainly couldn't be described as conservative. Its sides were cut out and it dipped low in the back.

They were as different as night and day. Their stepmother, Kathleen, had once described them as devil and angel with the roles reversed, Annette remembered, although it hadn't been a derogatory comment about either of them. It was simply that Marsha was so innocent, and Annette—she tended to *make* things happen rather than wait for them to occur. Occasionally that tendency got her into trouble, but she had always been clever enough to get herself out of it.

"Here." Annette offered the suntan oil to her sister. "You'd better use this before you turn into a lobster." Marsha had the dark complexion, but it was Annette who tanned easily.

"Thanks." Marsha set her book aside, laying it facedown opened to the page she was reading, to keep her place. As she began rubbing the oil on her arms, an expression of dreamy contentment swept over her face. "Isn't it beautiful here, Annette? I didn't think dad was serious when he said the family was going to spend our entire month's vacation at Wrightsville Beach."

"Why not?" Annette leaned back in the lounge chair and closed her eyes to bask in the sun.

"Well, when he's home he usually likes to stay in Delaware. It's really not surprising when you think about how much traveling he does," Marsha reasoned.

"True," she conceded. "But he also knows Kathleen has been stuck at home all while he's been gone. It's only natural that she'd like to get away for a while—especially now that Robby is older," she added, referring to their five-year-old half brother.

"You're right," Marsha agreed. "And as dad said, with both of us in college now, it's hard to say when we'll have another chance for the entire family to be together for a vacation again."

"I certainly intend to make the most of enjoying all this relaxation," Annette declared.

At the sound of approaching footsteps, Annette let her eyes open to mere slits and peered through her lashes. A uniformed waiter servicing the poolside area stopped next to Marsha's chair, an empty tray balanced on his uplifted palm. Annette made a swiftly astute appraisal of him. In his early twenties, the waiter was blond, tanned and very good-looking—and fully aware of the last.

"May I bring you ladies something to drink?" His flashing smile was intended to charm, and Marsha blushed faintly at its flirting quality.

Raising a hand to her forehead, Annette shielded her eyes from the glare of the sun. The movement immediately drew the waiter's attention to her as his admiring gaze skimmed the sleekness of her golden-tanned body and the provocative style of her swimsuit. Marsha was forgotten, a fact that didn't escape Annette's notice—or surprise her. His kind usually ran true to type, preferring fun-loving blondes to quiet brunettes.

"I'll have an iced tea," Annette ordered with a faintly inviting smile. Perhaps it wasn't fair to divert the handsome young man's attention from her sister, but it was a protective reaction. Marsha was so incredibly inexperienced when it came to handling men. She'd be way out of her league with this one.

"With lemon?" the waiter inquired, letting his expression show that he found Annette very attractive.

"Please." Annette let her smile increase to show she read his message, pretending to encourage even though he left her cold. Her glance ran to Marsha, who wasn't doing a very good job of masking her disappointment. "Do you want an iced tea, too?"

"Yes...please," she echoed Annette's order in a small voice.

"I'll be right back with your tea," the waiter promised. "If there's anything else you need, the name is Craig."

"I think the tea is all for now. Thank you, Craig," Annette murmured dryly.

With a mock bow he moved away to fill their order.

Annette rolled forward, draping an arm over an upraised knee to watch him go. She wasn't interested in him, but she knew Marsha was. For her sister's sake she wanted to be sure she had the young man's measure.

"Wasn't he gorgeous, Annette?" Marsha declared wistfully.

"Don't think lover boy doesn't know it, too," she inserted with dry cynicism. Craig took a little too much pride in his looks for her liking.

"How can you sound so indifferent?" her sister marveled. "I saw the way he looked at you. He went for you."

There was a lack of envy in Marsha's remark. She had become accustomed to men finding her older sister more attractive than herself.

"As you get older, Marsha, you'll learn that guys like Craig are in love with themselves," Annette explained patiently. "They think they're irresistible."

As she watched, the handsome waiter paused near another group of guests. One of the men in the small party caught her eye. Her pulse quickened with interest, her eyes lighting up. He was wearing a pair of black swimming trunks; the rest was all hard sun-bronzed flesh. The man was tall, a couple of inches over six feet, wide shoulders tapering to masculine slim hips.

As he turned slightly, Annette glimpsed the angular planes of his profile, slanted forehead, high-bridged nose and a strongly carved jawline. The sun's rays glinted on his dark brown hair, revealing its copper lights. Annette calculated that he was somewhere in the early thirties, a virile male specimen in his prime. Her glance strayed to his left hand, but there was no wedding ring—no jewelry at all, which meant absolutely nothing.

"I really don't understand how you can be so analytical about men," Marsha sighed. "Haven't you ever seen anyone that turned you on?"

Two minutes earlier Annette would have given her sister a negative reply. She had always been too intelligent to let her imagination run away with itself. At nineteen, almost twenty, she had dated a great deal, but she had never pretended even to herself that she was serious about any of the string of boyfriends. Annette had always been positive that she would instinctively know when she met the *right* man. And the signals were going off like crazy this very second.

"Yes," she said. "I have seen someone who turns me on. As a matter of fact, I'm looking at him right now," she informed her sister with calm certainty.

"What?" Marsha blinked at her, because it wasn't the anticipated answer. Her head swiveled to follow the direction of Annette's gaze. "Who?"

"The man in the black trunks." A thread of excitement ran through her nerve ends, tying them together.

Marsha looked. "Who is he?"

"I don't know—*yet*," Annette qualified her reply, because she was going to make it her business to find out. Her boldness always made Marsha uncomfortable. She felt her sister's uneasy glance on her.

"You don't know anything about him." It was almost an accusation.

Annette gave Marsha a look of indulgent patience. "But you can bet I'm going to find out."

Her gaze returned to the blatant sexuality of the stranger, so obviously male that he had no need to prove it. He was saying something to a female member of the group. Annette couldn't hear the words, but the slight breeze carried the husky timbre of his voice to her ears. She liked the sound of it as it shivered through her, like rough velvet drawn across her bare skin.

A uniformed figure crossed in front of her vision, briefly distracting her gaze. Annette recognized the blond waiter returning with their drinks. Her keen mind began working immediately. She welcomed him with a wide smile.

"That didn't take long," she remarked.

"It's all part of the service to keep the hotel

guests happy." His glance volunteered to go beyond the call of duty as he handed Marsha her glass and walked around the lounge chair to give Annette hers.

"Thank you." She set the glass down and reached for the check to sign it and charge it to the room. "Who is that man over there?" Annette asked with seemingly idle interest. "The one in the black trunks. He looks vaguely familiar, but I can't place where I've seen him," she lied.

"You must mean Joshua Lord," Craig replied.

Annette was careful to keep the focal point of her gaze on the waiter. The more attention she paid to him, the more information she'd get out of him. "Where have I heard that name before?" she wondered aloud, frowning.

"Among other things, he owns this resort. The Lords are one of North Carolina's old wealthy families," he explained, eager to impress Annette with his knowledge of the rich.

"Really," she murmured, and sent a glance in Joshua Lord's direction. His dark head was tipped attentively toward a bikini-clad redhead. "His wife is certainly a striking woman."

"That isn't his wife," Craig informed her, not noticing Annette's faint smile of satisfaction. "Josh isn't married. Judging by the variety of female visitors that have dined in his suite, he's too busy to settle down."

"I imagine all he has to do is crook his finger." Annette sipped at her glass of tea and smiled up at the waiter, matching his knowing grin. "You said he lives here at the hotel?"

"Yes,. he has a private suite."

"How convenient," she murmured with a throaty laugh.

"It certainly is," Craig agreed, but Annette was thinking how convenient it was for her, rather than the convenience of a hotel staff it provided for Joshua Lord.

One of the guests at poolside called out, summoning the waiter. His mouth crooked in a regretful smile. "Excuse me. I'll see you around."

"Bye." Annette watched him walk away, then let her gaze travel to Marsha. "Didn't I tell you I'd find out all about him?"

Marsha eyed her uncertainly, revealing the inner misgivings she had. "I don't know what you gained. Yes, you do know his name, where he lives and the fact that he isn't married, but a man like...Joshua Lord...can have practically any woman he wants. You said so yourself," Marsha reminded her. "What makes you think he'll be attracted to you?"

"Because I'm going to see that he is," Annette stated, and laughed softly at her sister's apprehensive expression. "Don't look so worried, Marsha," she admonished. "It will be easy."

"You've said that before." Marsha wasn't convinced.

"It's always worked out the way I wanted it to, hasn't it?" Annette reasoned.

"One of these times it won't," Marsha

warned. "And you're going to find yourself in big trouble."

Annette just laughed and sought out the object of her interest again. Various plans were already beginning to take shape in her mind and would need to be sorted through. There was more information she needed before she could settle on any one course of action. In the meantime she would have to be flexible.

As she watched, Joshua Lord detached himself from the group and walked toward the pool. He had an easy flowing stride, corded muscles rippling along his thigh and leg beneath sunbrowned flesh. There was a lazy confidence about his bearing, an aloof awareness of his surroundings.

The couple that had been cavorting in the pool earlier had climbed out to collapse in happy exhaustion on a couple of deck chairs. There was no one else in the pool when Josh Lord dived in. A second after he'd surfaced midway across the pool, Annette was reaching for her petaled swim cap.

"Where are you going?" Marsha asked, staring.

"For a swim," Annette replied with a confident gleam in her eyes. "You remember what Aunt Helen always said: don't wait for your ship to come in; swim out to meet it." She tucked the ends of her hair under the cap. "I'm on my way to meet *my ship*. Want to come?"

"No, thanks." Marsha picked up the book

she'd been reading. "Don't involve me in any of your schemes."

A faint smile played at the corners of Annette's mouth as she turned away and walked to the edge of the pool. Her sister's refusal was expected. Marsha wasn't very athletically oriented, preferring to be a spectator rather than a participant. Nothing was guaranteed to drive Annette crazy quicker than sitting on the sidelines. She was a natural competitor—and the higher the stakes, the more she enjoyed the game. A hint of danger just added to the excitement.

At the edge of the pool Annette paused to study the lone swimmer lapping the pool. She mentally timed the powerful stroke, but his pace was leisurely, which suited her purpose to a tee. Once he was clear of the immediate area, Annette arched and dived cleanly off the poolside, slicing into the water without a sound. She swam underwater for several yards and surfaced alongside him.

His brown eyes flicked over her in mild surprise. Up close, Annette could see the easy male charm in his strong features, a lazy sensuality lying in the chiseled lines. The potency of it heated her blood. She guessed how wide-eyed and innocent she looked as she blinked the water from her lashes.

"Hi." Annette spoke quickly before he could swim away. "Are you doing laps?"

"Yes." There was a faint narrowing of his gaze.

"Do you mind if I swim with you?" she asked, and offered the explanation, "It helps if I can pace myself against another swimmer."

"I don't mind." There was a glint of amusement in his dark eyes. He was used to women seeking him out. She would have to be very subtle.

"Good." Annette struck out for the far end of the pool with a clean strong stroke.

All the hours she'd spent training on the college swim team were about to pay off. But not yet. Annette didn't attempt to outdistance him or even increase the pace he'd been swimming previously. She wasn't foolish enough to believe she could outswim him even with her expertise in the water, but she could make him take notice of her—eventually. First she wanted to settle into a rhythm; the tempo could always be increased later.

For the entire length of the pool, Annette remained even with him, fully aware that he was holding back the same as she was—only he didn't know that. With each breath she looked at the dark-haired swimmer opposite her and the cleaving strokes of his muscled arms.

At the end of the first lap she did a racer's turn, not trying for speed. She was a half length in front of him, the maneuver catching him off guard. This time Annette didn't try to take advantage of it as he quickly caught up with her. When their eyes met briefly on a mutually timed breath, there was a gleam of respect in his. Annette turned her face into the water and effectively hid her smile. He picked up the tempo slightly and she stayed with him.

She counted the laps, concentrating on her stroke. Past experience had taught her that she lost her kick after a mile. She waited until she had only two lengths of the pool left to go, then she made her move, putting everything she had into the turn and launching herself off the side of the pool. She was more than a length ahead of him when she surfaced and struck out for the other side at race tempo.

Before Annette made the final turn he had caught up with her, as she had known he would. But she had his full attention. Nothing attracted it quicker from a man than to have a female challenge his male superiority. She would have thrown the race in order to let him win, but it wasn't necessary.

On the last lap he was easily outdistancing her. Annette used every ounce of her reserve strength to keep respectably close. The instant her hand touched the side of the pool she stopped, even though he continued. Her lungs felt ready to burst.

With the assistance of the water's buoyancy, she levered herself out of the pool with her arms, swinging her legs out of the water to recline at right angles to the edge. Annette drank in gulps of air, her breasts heaving with the effort to fill her lungs. Pulling off the swim cap that had kept her hair half-dry, she leaned backward on her elbows'. Her head was thrown back, exposing the curve of her throat and catching the sheen of the sunlight in her blond hair.

"Are you quitting?" It was a taunting challenge, and Annette half turned, one elbow supporting her weight. Josh Lord was treading water, eyeing her exhausted state with male complacency, even white teeth showing against sunbronzed skin.

For a brief instant she was irritated to see he was barely breathing hard at all, but the feeling was forgotten as his gaze traveled over the curves of her figure, lingering a scant second on the swell of her breasts.

"Yes," Annette admitted in a voice that was attractively breathless. "A mile is my limit. Thanks for the workout."

"Anytime, kid." He turned in the water and swam leisurely away, missing the look of shock, then anger, that swept through Annette's expression.

Kid! With a sudden surge of energy she rolled to her feet and crossed to the lounge chair next to Marsha's. Her temper was simmering at a low boil. So he thought she was a kid! The light of battle stormed in her gray eyes.

"What happened?" Marsha recognized that look and inwardly trembled at what it might mean. "Did it backfire?"

"Not exactly." Annette stretched out in the lounge chair to let the sun dry her, closing her eyes. "I accomplished what I set out to do."

Namely, to get Josh Lord to notice her, and she had succeeded in that. But at the moment, this "kid" had to do some rethinking. It would be simply too immature to tell him that she would be twenty in just a few days.

Through slitted eyes Annette observed him climbing out of the pool a few minutes later. His wet hair gleamed almost black, its burnished highlights temporarily hidden. The sheen of moisture on his flatly muscled body gave his deeply tanned flesh a polished look. His hard male physique started a quivering sensation in her stomach as Annette imagined what it would be like to be next to it.

He draped a towel around his neck but made no effort to dry himself. When he cast a glance in her direction, Annette was glad her eyes appeared to be closed. She didn't want to be caught watching him. A ripple of satisfaction eliminated any lingering irritation. Even if he considered her a "kid," he was aware of her. For the time being she was willing to settle for that.

As Josh Lord left the poolside area to disappear down one of the walkways, Marsha laid her book down. "Here come dad and Kathleen. Robby must have finally woken up from his afternoon nap."

Annette sat up as her father and stepmother approached, a black-haired little boy tugging impatiently at Kathleen's hand to hurry her. She smiled, liking the picture the three of them made with her father's arm possessively around the shoulders of the attractive auburn-haired woman. It was always reassuring to see how much in love the two of them were.

Marsha waved to attract the couple's attention and Kathleen released her son's hand. Robby careered past the other chairs, a pint-size cyclone in swimming trunks as he raced toward Marsha and Annette.

"Whoa!" Annette laughed and caught her half brother around the waist to stop him. "You're not supposed to run around the pool. Sometimes it's slick and you'll fall."

Her bathing suit was still wet, and Robby noticed it immediately. "How come you didn't wait until I woke up to go swimming?" he accused. "I'd wait for you."

"Get your water wings and I'll go swimming again—with you," Annette promised, and turned him loose.

Robby barely gave Kathleen a chance to set the beach bag down before he was diving into it. "Not so fast," she admonished him for the careless regard toward the other items in the oversize bag. "Fold the towels you dumped out."

"I'll do it, Kathleen," Marsha volunteered.

"No, Robby can do it." The rejection was accompanied by a smile. "You girls spoil him too much as it is."

"I thought that was what older sisters were supposed to do," Annette laughed. "Marsha and I will watch him so you and dad can have some time together." She glanced at her father, so tall and handsome, and looked into a pair of gray eyes the same color as hers. "Besides, we don't want Robby giving dad any more gray hairs." She teased him about the white strand she'd found mixed in among the black the day before.

"Don't blame those on Robby," Jordan Long replied. "If anyone in this family is capable of giving me gray hairs, it's you, Annette."

"When have you ever had to worry about me?" she chided.

"Practically since the day you were born," he retorted dryly. "Speaking of which—have you decided what you want for your birthday?"

"Yes." She had an instant image of Joshua Lord.

"What?" Kathleen prompted while she adjusted the water wings on Robby's arms.

"A Ferrari," Annette lied. She couldn't very well tell her father what she really wanted for her birthday.

"Try again," he suggested, and Annette laughed, knowing full well that her request had been out of the question.

CHAPTER TWO

ANNETTE ROLLED OVER in the bed and felt the glare of an early-morning sun on her eyes. She pulled the blankets over her head in an attempt to shut it out, but it was no use. Her sleep had been disrupted, and once awake, she was rarely able to go back to sleep.

With a groan she tossed back the covers and turned to look at the occupant of the room's other single bed. Marsha was sound asleep. Annette wanted to throw a pillow at her out of sheer envy, but it wasn't her sister's fault that she was awake. She crawled out of bed and padded into the bathroom.

A few minutes later she emerged, her teeth brushed and the tiredness washed from her eyes. Before deciding what to wear, Annette walked to the window to see what kind of day it promised to be. Except for a few innocent white clouds, the sky was bright and clear.

The second-floor window provided a view of the bay and the golf course that adjoined the resort-hotel complex. From this vantage point Annette studied other early-morning risers out jogging. A lone runner stood out from the others.

She'd recognize that length of muscled leg and that flowing stride anywhere. That well-trimmed male body had to be Josh Lord's.

Her gaze skipped ahead of him to study his possible routes and instantly memorized them. Turning quickly from the window, she hurried to the dresser drawers containing her clothes. She pawed carelessly through the folded clothes until she found her turquoise blue jogging shorts and matching tank top. In record time Annette peeled off her T-shirt-styled nightgown and donned the jogging outfit, not bothering with a bra.

When she reached for a pair of heavy socks to wear with her running shoes, Annette caught a glimpse of her reflection in the dresser's mirror. She paused to look more closely. Her face was scrubbed clean of any makeup, the result combining with her clothes to make her appear more youthful.

"A kid, huh?" she murmured at her reflection, and studied her shoulder-length blond hair. Reaching up, Annette loosely bunched one side of her hair in a pigtail style. Wicked mischief gleamed in her eyes. "If he thought I looked like a kid yesterday, just wait until he sees me this morning."

Leaving the socks behind, she dashed into the bathroom to fix her hair, securing the sides with rubber bands. The result was positively juvenile—and she laughed out loud. Returning to the bedroom area she shared with her sister, Annette tugged on her socks and shoes.

"What are you doing?" Marsha's sleepy voice asked. "What time is it?"

"A little after six." With one shoe tied, Annette shifted position to tie the laces of the other.

Marsha frowned in her effort to focus her eyes on Annette. "You aren't going to run at this hour?" She protested against the thought of such strenuous activity so early in the morning.

"Yep," Annette answered brightly, and shot her sister a glittering look. "You never know who I might 'run' into."

"Let me guess," Marsha replied dryly, and sank back to her bed.

"Wish me luck." Annette started toward the door.

"With him you'll need it," Marsha called after her.

As Annette descended the stairs to the ground floor, she silently conceded that in this instance her sister might be right. Luck would come in handy in catching Josh Lord. Without a second glance she trotted past the azalea bushes and their exotic pink blossoms. Playing a hunch, Annette headed toward the hotel's beach on the Atlantic Ocean.

Choosing the sidewalk instead of the sand, she rounded the curve of the bathhouses. Her heart did a funny little leap when she recognized the man jogging toward her. The sleeves of a sweat shirt were tied around his neck, baring the muscled wall of his flat stomach, his tanned flesh glistening with perspiration. Annette saw the answering glint of recognition in his dark eyes when they spied her. He didn't even appear to be surprised to see her jogging.

"It's a gorgeous morning, isn't it?" she greeted him, and deliberately shifted her course so she would pass him on the beach side of the walk. So far everything was going perfectly.

"It is," he agreed with a faint nod, not breaking stride.

Annette didn't slacken her pace, either. But as she drew level with him to jog by, she deliberately stepped off the sidewalk onto the soft sand, throwing herself off balance on purpose. She faked a startled cry and tumbled to the ground, the sand cushioning her fall. Very careful not to look around, she grabbed for her ankle and inwardly held her breath.

"Are you hurt?" His inquiry nearly had her leaping into the air, but she managed to contain the surge of triumph. There had been a skeptical note in his voice, as if he guessed the fall was for his benefit.

She cast him a quick glance and immediately lowered her head. She didn't feel ready to hold his steady gaze. "I'm okay," Annette insisted, and flexed her ankle with feigned care. "I just turned it."

"Are you sure?" He waited, as if sensing something wasn't altogether right about this.

"Yes," Annette nodded, but kept her face averted as she shifted her legs under her as if to rise, then paused to brush away the grains of sand clinging to her bare arms and legs. Satisfaction warmed her blood at the sound of his approaching footsteps in the sand.

"Let me give you a hand up." A large sunbrowned hand was extended to her.

She looked at it, then glanced hesitantly at his shrewdly inspecting gaze before she tentatively placed her hand in his grip. "It's embarrassing," Annette murmured as he helped her to her feet, conscious of his strength. He wasn't going to be easy to fool.

"What is?" he inquired.

"Falling down," she explained with a crooked smile of chagrin. "Nobody can do it gracefully, and you always feel like a stumbling fool." The pretense of candor was a direct gambit to throw him off track. Annette knew she had succeeded when she saw the amused indulgence in his expression. He released her hand but didn't let go of her, shifting his grip to support her elbow.

"It happens to all of us at one time or another," he assured her, then suggested, "Why don't you test that ankle?"

She took a tentative step, deliberately favoring it. "It's a little tender, but I can walk it off." Annette wasn't about to pretend it was anything more than a simple turn. As she stood so close to him, his body heat was giving off a heady male odor that stimulated her senses, which were already overly alert to his presence. Her sideglance caught his watchful look, a degree of suspicion lingering.

"It's bound to be weak. I wouldn't run on it this morning," he advised.

"No, I don't suppose I should," she sighed the agreement. Since she no longer needed his support, his hand fell away. "Thanks for stopping—" Annette paused and looked at him expectantly to see if he would supply his name.

"Josh," he filled in her apparent blank.

"Annette," she identified herself, and reached out to seal the introduction with a handshake. When she didn't immediately withdraw her hand from the warm clasp of his fingers, Josh continued to hold it loosely. She wished there was something she could do to erase that glint of amusement from his eyes, but for the time being she had to let it remain. "Thanks, Josh."

"My pleasure." His smile was brief.

Drawing her hand back, she took a deep breath, which stretched the knit material of her tank top across the jutting curves of her breasts. The action attracted his attention. A flicker of annoyance appeared briefly in his eyes. Annette wanted to laugh, because she knew he regarded her as a mere child and felt guilty for looking at her "budding" femininity. His gaze ran sharply back to her face, as if he guessed she had deliberately attracted his notice.

"Can I buy you some orange juice or a cup of coffee?" Annette offered. For a split second she thought he was going to refuse.

"Coffee sounds good. I haven't had my morning cup yet," Josh accepted, and untied the sleeves of his sweat shirt. She was almost sorry when he pulled it over his head to put it on. It seemed a sin to cover up such a virile chest.

Her expression must have betrayed part of her thoughts, because he tipped his head to one side. "Is something wrong?"

Annette started to deny it, then let a precocious smile touch her mouth. "I was just thinking this is the first time I've seen you with a shirt on."

Just for an instant he looked irritated, then he chuckled in his throat. "It is, isn't it?" He spread his fingers between her shoulder blades to push her forward. "I take it that you are staying here at the hotel?"

"Yes." She moved in the direction of the bath-houses, where there was a walkway leading around the tall fence that screened the swimming pool from the beach. "Are you staying at the hotel, too?" she asked, as if she didn't already know.

"Yes." But Josh Lord failed to mention his status as owner of the resort. "I believe they'll serve us outside on the patio if you'd like to sit there."

"That would be nice," Annette agreed to the suggestion, warmly conscious of his fingers touching the bare skin of her shoulders.

"Where's your home?" Josh asked, and guided her around the pool to the umbrella-shaded tables outside the coffee shop.

"Delaware, just outside Dover." Her skin felt cool when he took his hand away to pull out a wrought-iron chair for her to sit on.

"That's up the coast a few miles," he remarked, waiting until she was seated before he sat down, his long legs nearly touching hers. "Is this your first trip to North Carolina?"

"Yes. We flew in a couple of days ago. So far we haven't done much sight-seeing, but we have a whole month." Annette disliked his questions. They were too simple—too polite. She wouldn't get anywhere this way.

"We?" Josh inquired blandly.

"My family—dad, my stepmother, Kathleen, my sister, Marsha, my little brother, Rob, and myself." Annette knew it made her seem even younger to be vacationing with her family. She took impish glee in naming them all. "Where's your home?"

"Here. I'm a native Tar Heel." Josh looked up as Annette heard a set of footsteps approach the table. She glanced over her shoulder and recognized the blond-haired waiter walking toward their table. It was Craig, the one who had flirted with her at the pool the previous afternoon. He appeared startled to see her, whether because she was with Josh Lord or because of her juvenile hairstyle, Annette couldn't tell.

"Hello, Craig." She greeted him with a good deal more familiarity than their short acquaintanceship warranted. "You must have the early shift today."

"I do," he admitted, and darted a curious glance at Josh, whose gaze had narrowed slightly. "Did you want something?"

"Yes, I'll have a cup of black coffee," Annette

ordered, and looked all innocent-eyed at Josh.

"The same," he echoed.

"Two black coffees coming right up," Craig nodded, then backed away. He seemed a little uneasy under Josh's narrow regard.

When the waiter had gone Annette was subjected to his silent scrutiny. "Do you know him?" he inquired.

"Do you mean Craig?" she asked unnecessarily, then shrugged. "I met him yesterday at the pool."

The line of his mouth slanted in amusement. "You were busy yesterday at the pool, weren't you?"

She gave him a blank look. "What do you mean?" Then she pretended to realize. "Oh, because I met you there, too. I guess my sister, Marsha, is the shy one in our family."

"It wouldn't hurt to be cautious," Josh stated. "I wouldn't get too friendly with Craig if I were you." But Annette wasn't sure whether he was really warning her away from Craig or himself.

"Why not?" She cocked her head to one side. It was very hard for her to keep a straight face.

"He runs with a pretty fast crowd," he replied. "And you're a little young to be getting involved with college-aged boys."

"Oh." Annette had to lower her chin to keep her smile from showing. It was extremely difficult not to inform him that she would be a junior when she entered college that autumn. But she simply couldn't resist asking him, "How old do you think I am, Josh?"

There was a slight hesitation before he said, "Seventeen." He even sounded skeptical about that.

"Really?" She faked a disappointed look.

"Yes." He didn't succeed too well at hiding his smile at her response. "Why?"

"I thought I looked older," Annette shrugged. "At least twenty."

"Don't rush it," Josh advised, his mouth twisting wryly. "You'll get there soon enough."

"Yes, I guess I will." *A lot sooner than you think,* she added to herself.

Craig came back, carrying two mugs of coffee.

"Put it on my tab," Josh instructed to dismiss him.

"But it was supposed to be my treat," Annette protested as Craig slipped away, unwilling to wait around while she argued with the owner. "I invited you."

"I'd forgotten," he lied. "Next time you can buy."

"Okay." She gave in readily to the suggestion even though she knew he didn't mean it that there might be a next time. She took a sip of the steaming coffee. "Do you mind if I ask how old you are?"

"No. I'm thirty-three." When she laughed he arched an eyebrow. "Did I say something funny?"

"Not really," Annette assured him. "It's just

the advice you were passing out a while ago sounded like something from my father. And I didn't think you were his age." She flirted a little. "You aren't that much older than I am."

"Enough older, Annette," he countered, but his gaze skimmed her. She knew he wasn't completely indifferent to her feminine attributes, age difference or no.

"What kind of business are you in?" She discreetly changed the subject, taking a drink of the coffee.

"Real estate." Which encompassed a lot of territory. "What does your father do?"

"He's a troubleshooter for an oil company. He gets sent to all the hot spots."

"Sounds like he does a lot of traveling," Josh suggested.

"He does," Annette readily agreed. "That's why the whole family vacations together when he's home. We don't get to see very much of him for most of the year."

Craig approached their table again with a pot of coffee. Josh covered his cup with his hand. "No more for me."

"Me, neither," Annette refused. She sensed that Josh intended to bring their meeting to a close, and she wanted to be the one to do it. "I have to be getting back to the room before dad starts wondering where I am."

"I have a business appointment," Josh admitted, and pushed his chair away from the table.

"Have a good day," she wished him, standing up to leave, too.

"You, too." His smile stiffened a little at the last, then he was moving away.

Annette was slower to leave, savoring the experience. She didn't notice that Craig was lingering on the sidelines until he came forward to carry away their coffee cups. He glanced in the direction that Josh had disappeared, then looked curiously at Annette.

"You thought you recognized him yesterday," he remarked. "I guess it turned out that you had met him before."

"No." She shook her head in a brief denial. "We just happened to run into each other while we were out jogging this morning and decided to have coffee together."

"You work pretty fast," he commented with a trace of jealous sarcasm.

Annette smiled. "I've heard that you do, too."

Craig straightened, suddenly uncertain if he had misunderstood. He was conceited enough to believe Annette was still interested in him. His manner changed to winning charm. "A friend of mine is throwing a party tonight. Are you free?"

"I'm afraid not," she refused the offhand invitation.

"Maybe another time," he suggested with renewed hope.

"Maybe another time," Annette agreed, sincerely doubting that it would ever come. She turned to leave, tossing an airy "See you!" over her shoulder. But as she started through the breezeway between the hotel buildings, she met her father and Kathleen.

"Good morning," her father greeted her, and let his gaze slide past her to Craig. "I see you've already made a conquest in the short time you've been here. And you wonder where the gray hairs come from," he mocked.

"If you mean Craig, I'm not interested," Annette retorted, but she was relieved her father hadn't arrived a few minutes earlier and seen her with Josh. She had the uneasy feeling he wouldn't have approved. Right now it was better that he didn't know about him. She pretended to scan the black hair at his temples for a silver strand. "Did you find another gray hair this morning, dad?"

"No. Surprised?" he countered.

"No." Annette laughed, then glanced at Kathleen. "Where's Robby?"

"Marsha is getting him dressed," Kathleen replied, explaining her son's absence. "We were just going into the coffee shop for breakfast. Do you want to join us?"

Annette was tempted to accept the invitation, but she knew they didn't have many chances to be alone. "I think I'll change first."

"We're going to Orton Plantation later on this morning, so wear your walking shoes," her father warned.

"I will," she promised with a smile, and started off for the room she shared with her sister.

The door was standing open when she reached

the room. Robby was sitting patiently on an unmade bed while Marsha knelt to tie his shoes.

"H'lo, Annette," he greeted her loudly when she entered the room.

"Good morning," Annette replied.

Marsha glanced at her and observed, "You're smiling like the Cheshire cat."

"Is that a complaint or a compliment?" Annette laughed.

"I just don't understand how you get away with some of the things you do," her sister replied, and set Robby on the floor.

"What does Annette get away with?" he wanted to know.

"Nothing that your ears need to hear about," Marsha retorted, then turned her attention back to Annette. "I guess your mission was accomplished. You ran into him?"

"I practically fell at his feet—literally." She made an exaggerated show of limping across the room, favoring her ankle.

"You didn't fake a sprained ankle," Marsha accused.

"No, just a little twist, but it got me a cup of coffee," Annette declared with twinkling triumph.

"Have you ever given any thought to what will happen when he finds out about your little tricks?" Marsha shook her head in disapproval.

"When who finds out?" Robby twisted his head back to look up at his sister. "Daddy?"

"No, pet," Annette assured him. "Marsha

and I are talking about someone else. Personally I can hardly wait for the day that he finds out the truth."

Marsha frowned. "Why?" She knew her sister too well to trust Annette in her present impish mood.

"Because he's convinced I'm seventeen," Annette grinned.

"Did you tell him that?" Marsha squeaked, and stared at the childish pigtails. "Is that why you're wearing your hair like that?"

"I didn't tell him I was seventeen," Annette said. "He guessed that's how old I was."

"Why didn't you tell him the truth?"

"Because he wouldn't have believed me, so I didn't try to convince him differently," Annette shrugged.

"So who is going to tell him?" Marsha asked, then recoiled. "I told you I didn't want to become involved in this."

"I remember." Annette sauntered to the closet to choose her clothes for the day.

"Please don't forget it." It went against Marsha's nature to stay upset for long. She disliked arguments or anything that remotely resembled a battle of words. Her tone became placating. "Robby and I haven't had breakfast yet. Would you like us to wait for you while you change?"

"Will the restaurant have my favorite cereal?" Robby asked. "That's what I want this morning."

"It'll only take me a few minutes to change.

Why don't I meet you at the coffee shop?" Annette suggested, because it was apparent her little brother was becoming impatient.

"Let's do that, Marsha," he urged.

"Okay. We'll see you there," she told Annette, and took Robby's hand.

"Close the door on your way out," Annette called as she slipped a pair of white slacks off a hanger.

CHAPTER THREE

THE LOCK DEFIED ANNETTE'S ATTEMPTS to turn the key she'd inserted in it. Hot, tired and impatient, she jiggled it angrily and tugged at the doorknob. Strands of sun-blond hair had escaped the confining elastic bands securing her pigtails. Perspiration plastered them against her neck and made the tank top to her jogging suit stick to her back.

When the lock resisted another attempt, Annette hit the hotel-room door with the flat of her hand in a fit of pique. She would have kicked it if her right foot didn't hurt so much from the blister on its heel. Her irritable mood was caused by more than just heat and fatigue. Frustration contributed a healthy amount to it.

As she yanked the key out of the keyhole to start all over again, the door swung open. For a stunned instant Annette thought it had opened of its own accord, until she saw her bathrobed sister modestly using the bulwark of the door as a shield.

"If you forgot your key, why didn't you just knock instead of rattling the doorknob like that?" Marsha complained with a trace of lingering anxiety. "I thought someone was trying to break in."

"I didn't forget my key!" Annette snapped, and limped across the threshold, a raw pain burning where her running shoe rubbed the heel of her right foot. She aimed her body for the nearest chair. "The damned thing wouldn't work!"

"What happened? Did you sprain your ankle for real this time?" Marsha asked as she closed the door and Annette flopped in the chair by the window.

"No, I didn't," Annette sighed at the implied criticism. "I have a blister."

She untied her shoe and eased it off her foot, feeling the first glimmer of relief. There was still a sock to be removed, which produced a hissing breath of pain when she rolled it off. As Annette twisted her foot across a knee to examine it, Marsha bent toward it, too, and grimaced in sympathy.

"It looks sore," she murmured.

"You ought to feel it from this end," Annette grumbled as the inflamed area throbbed with the exposure to air.

"Do you want me to get you a Band-Aid or something?" Marsha offered.

"No. It will be okay." She leaned back in the chair and let it support her head. Her mouth thinned into a disgruntled line. "Three days of jogging every morning, and this blister is all I have to show for it."

"You didn't see him this morning, either," Marsha gathered from her remark.

"I saw him all right," Annette admitted with frustration, "but from three blocks away. I couldn't catch up with him—not with this blister."

Marsha sat on the single bed opposite the chair and folded her hands in her lap. "Did it occur to you that this might be a sign you should give up?" she suggested.

"No, it didn't occur to me." Annette chewed thoughtfully on a finger, her mind working feverishly. "I'm just going to have to think of some other way to see him."

"You've jogged every morning and haunted the swimming pool every afternoon," her sister reminded her. "Maybe it just isn't meant to be."

"I can't accept that," Annette stated with a decisive shake of her head. "This is where you and I differ, Marsha. You're content to just sit back and wait for Mr. Right to *happen* along, certain that he'll take one look at you and whisk you off to the altar. That isn't the way it works," she insisted. "God helps those who help themselves. You have to make your own opportunities."

On certain things, Marsha could be stubborn. This was one of them. "But you can't *make* somebody love you, Annette. Either he does or he doesn't."

"Look." Annette leaned forward, feeling that she was explaining the facts of life to a child instead of her nearly adult sister. "Josh has looked at me. He's interested. I know that. The seed has been planted and it just needs some water to make it grow." She paused. "The difference between you and me is that you'll wait until it rains—if it ever does. And I'm going to make sure it gets water if I have to carry it myself!"

Marsha didn't attempt to deny the accuracy of her sister's assessment. "But you're practically chasing him. I don't think it looks right."

"Marsha, be realistic." Annette contained her exasperation to appeal to her sister's common sense. "It's the oldest game around. A boy chases a girl until she catches him, don't you know that? You and I are the only ones who know that I'm chasing Josh Lord. You can bet I'm not going to let him find it out. He's going to think it's all his idea."

"But you're tricking him into thinking that, and it isn't fair," she protested.

Annette sighed and shook her head. "All's fair in love and war—haven't you heard that before, either?"

"Yes, I've heard it," Marsha retorted in a rare moment of irritability. "Sometimes, Annette, I think you keep a file of all these sayings so you can drag out whatever one happens to apply to a situation so you can justify what you're doing."

For a minute Annette just stared at her, a little dumbfounded. Finally she said, "You are my sister, Marsha, and I love you dearly. There isn't anything I wouldn't do for you." She paused and gave a baffled shake of her head. "But sometimes it's hard for me to believe that anyone so incredibly naive could be related to me. Marsha, you are really priceless at times."

Marsha drew back to eye her sister in confusion. "Why?"

"Because you are sitting here lecturing me about chasing men—as if I have a long history of pursuing them. Have you ever known me to do it before?" Annette questioned.

"No," she admitted with a lame shrug. Annette had always been popular with boys. Marsha couldn't recall a single time when her sister had stayed home for the lack of a date, but neither could she remember Annette's actively seeking a boy out.

"Doesn't that convince you that Josh is a special case?" Annette reasoned.

"I guess so." Marsha found herself agreeing and silently marveled at her sister's knack of twisting people around to her way of thinking. She was incredibly persuasive.

"Then, instead of being so negative, why don't you come up with some constructive suggestions?" Annette appealed for her help. "Girls are always accidentally-on-purpose turning up where the boys are. I haven't had much luck lately at the swimming pool or the jogging path, so I'd really appreciate some new ideas."

Marsha thought for a minute, then offered, "What about where he works? Does he have an office somewhere?"

"He not only has an office, he has an entire office building," Annette informed her with an expression of futility. "I made a couple of discreet inquiries and got the address from the hotel operator. Yesterday morning I hired a taxi and went by it. That's why I was late meeting you guys," she explained.

"And?" Marsha prompted.

"And the building sits there all by itself, practically," Annette sighed. "There isn't a single shop or store within three blocks of it. I wouldn't have a believable excuse for being there. It isn't a place you just 'happened by.'"

"It doesn't sound like it," she murmured. "If we eliminate the office, what else is there? We know he jogs and swims. What about other hobbies or sports?"

Annette brightened at the question and nibbled at her lip. "I think you're on the right track," she murmured.

"Maybe he plays golf," Marsha suggested. "There's a course adjacent to the hotel."

"He probably does. The problem is, I don't," she said with a rueful smile. "And I'm not about to volunteer to caddy for him." She snapped her fingers. "I've got it! The tennis courts here at the hotel! Josh is bound to play!"

She bounded out of the chair, mindless of her aching heel, and rushed over with one shoe off and one shoe on to hug her sister. "If it hadn't been for you, I might not have thought of it. Thanks!"

"How does that help?" Marsha didn't understand and frowned at Annette as she hobbled away from her. "You can't spend all your time hanging around the tennis courts waiting for him to show up."

Midway to the bathroom and its shower, Annette halted to explain, "That's the best part. I don't have to hang around the tennis courts. Anybody who wants to play has to reserve the use of the court. All I have to do is get a peek at the reservation list and I'll know the exact day and time Josh will be there."

It sounded simple, but Marsha knew better. "And just how do you intend to get a look at that reservation list?"

"If you get dressed while I shower, you can come with me and I'll show you," Annette declared on an infectious note of confidence.

MARSHA WAS HALF-CONVINCED that her older sister was a bulldozer made out of velvet. Somehow Annette managed to push obstacles aside as if they didn't exist. For the past ten minutes she had been talking to the tennis pro on duty about the selection of times the courts were available in the next few days—talking and joking with him as if they were old friends, that is.

When the phone in the tennis shop rang, Annette casually turned the reservation book around so she could read it, and smiled at the pro. "Go ahead and answer that. I'll look over these free times and decide which one we want to reserve."

He agreed without any hesitation and moved to the end of the counter to pick up the phone. Annette slid a twinkling glance of triumph at Marsha and began looking over the list. Josh Lord's name practically leaped off the page across from the five o'clock slot the next afternoon.

When Marsha noticed that the court next to the one Josh had reserved wasn't booked, she murmured in a low undertone, "You lead a charmed life, Annette."

"I do, don't I?" Annette admitted that luck played an important role on this occasion. The subject was shelved as the tennis pro hung up the phone and came back. "Mark me down for tomorrow afternoon at four-thirty." She gave him her name and room number. "And we'll need to rent some tennis balls and rackets."

"Sure thing," he nodded. "Any preference in equipment?"

"No." Annette shook her head with indifference. "Whatever you have on hand is fine. Marsha and I aren't particular." She pushed away from the counter to leave while Marsha stared at her in openmouthed astonishment. "See you tomorrow."

They were outside on the sidewalk before Marsha recovered her voice. "When did I say anything about playing tennis?"

"I took it for granted that you would," Annette admitted, a little startled that her sister appeared unwilling. "It's a trifle difficult to play tennis by yourself. What did you think I was going to do?"

"I thought you were just going to find out when Josh was going to be there, then drop by," she replied.

"What would I do? Watch him play?" Annette scoffed. "That's a bit obvious, Marsha. If I'm playing tennis I have a reason to be there—and he can't be sure I'm only there to see him."

"But I told you I didn't want to get involved in any of your schemes," Marsha reminded her.

"All you're going to do is play tennis, for heaven's sake!" she declared in mild exasperation, shaking her head.

"But I know the way you work," Marsha countered. "It all starts out so innocent. You involve people on the very edges of your plans—and before they know it they're in over their heads."

"You're exaggerating, Marsha," she dismissed the statement.

"No, I'm not," her sister replied with the certainty that came from past experience. "Even if Joshua Lord notices you tomorrow, I don't see what good it's going to do you. He thinks you're seventeen. He isn't going to take you seriously until he finds out you're older. You really should tell him before it goes any further."

Annette stopped, striving for patience. "And just what am I supposed to do? Should I walk up to him and whip out my driver's license, birth certificate and passport, then say, 'Look, Josh, I'll be twenty in four more days'?"

"How will you tell him?" Marsha asked, since that was obviously not her sister's choice.

"I'm not sure yet," she admitted. "At the moment, being seventeen in his eyes is an advantage."

Marsha frowned. "I missed something. How is it an advantage?"

"I wouldn't even want to try to guess how many twenty-year-old girls he's dated in his lifetime, but how often do you think he's been attracted to a supposedly seventeen-year-old girl? Right now I stand out in a crowd. I'm not just another blonde in his life," Annette explained.

"I hadn't thought of it that way," her sister admitted.

"I have." Annette started walking again. She was wearing backless sandals so she wouldn't aggravate the blistered sore on her right heel. "And that's the reason I don't mind being seventeen for a while longer." She paused, then said, "Since I failed to ask you earlier, will you play tennis with me tomorrow?"

Marsha glanced at her and smiled ruefully. "I don't know why you bothered to ask. You know I will—although I probably need my head examined for agreeing."

THE HOURS Annette had spent at the swimming pool had tanned her skin a rich golden color and added a few platinum streaks to her hair. The result was a perfect foil for her short white tennis outfit with its black trim. Annette had deliberately booked the adjacent court a half hour earlier than Josh, so she would be there playing when he arrived. Her side of the net allowed her to face the direction that he would come.

As the time grew closer for Josh to arrive, she started getting nervous, wondering if he'd canceled or changed the hour. She nearly missed the easy lob from Marsha and tried to bring her attention back to the uneven game. They were in the middle of a set when Annette saw Josh approaching the court, accompanied by one of the hotel's tennis pros. Her heart did a little tumble at the sight of him in white tennis shorts and a knit shirt stretched tautly across his chest. The sun glinted copper bright on his dark hair.

A faintly bemused smile played at the corners of his hard mouth when Josh recognized her. Annette smashed Marsha's lob to the opposite corner, scoring an easy point.

"That's game!" she declared, even though it wasn't, and trotted around the net to take a break and change sides.

"Are you sure?" Marsha frowned, standing flat-footed at the baseline. "I thought it—"

"That's game," Annette repeated, and quelled her sister's protest with a silencing look. Marsha glanced around, noting Josh's arrival for the first time.

"I guess you're right." She understood the reason for Annette's unusual scoring and didn't dispute the claim.

Annette walked to the corner near the high fence of green mesh and picked up the towel she'd left with her things. She pretended to wipe away nonexistent perspiration from her face and neck as Josh, in the next court, unzipped the case protecting his racket. Tension licked along her nerve ends while she waited for him to glance her way. When he did turn his dark gaze toward her, the chiseled planes of his face seemed to fill her vision to the exclusion of anything else.

"Fancy meeting you here." She feigned a mild surprise to see him.

"I have the strange feeling that you're following me," Josh remarked with an astutely sweeping glance. "I wonder why that is?"

"I was just going to accuse you of following me," Annette countered with a husky laugh. "I was here first."

"Appearances can be deceiving." He wasn't convinced.

Annette decided that the best way to allay his suspicions was to confront them. "I'm not about to deny that I think you're a very attractive man." The way he was affecting her practically made it an understatement. Her stomach was all tied in knots and it felt as if her heart were in her throat. "But I guess I'm a little old-fashioned."

"Oh?" The raised eyebrow asked for an explanation of that comment.

"Yes. You see, I prefer a man to do the chasing." Annette's smoke-colored eyes looked at him with absolute innocence as she turned away while she was still in possession of the last word. She walked back to her court and called across the net to Marsha. "Are you ready?" At the affirmative nod from her sister, she batted the ball to her. "It's your service."

Annette had a difficult time concentrating on her game. She was more interested in the tennis match being played on the adjacent court. Marsha was an adequate player, but she wasn't a challenging opponent. And Josh was a powerful distraction.

The match ended with Annette the easy winner. She would have liked to stay and watch Josh, but as she had pointed out to Marsha yesterday, it was simply too obvious. Plus, she was plagued by the knowledge this hadn't been a very successful meeting. As she and Marsha gathered their things to leave, Annette tried to think of a way to salvage something from this missed opportunity.

Her glance lighted on Marsha's tennis sweater, a twin to her own except that hers was trimmed in black and Marsha's had navy blue braid. She froze for an instant as an idea formed.

"Marsha, is your room key in your sweater pocket?" Annette asked with an eager rush.

"Yes. Why?" Marsha was absently curious. "Did you forget yours?"

"No, I have mine," Annette assured her. "As we leave the courts I want you to accidentally drop your sweater. You can't know that you dropped it."

"Then why am I doing it?" Marsha frowned.

"Because I want you to leave it behind—with the key in it—so Josh can find it when he leaves, and return it," Annette explained.

"You can't be serious." Marsha stared at her, fully aware that Annette was perfectly serious. "I came along with you this afternoon just to play tennis. You didn't say anything about losing my sweater."

"Marsha, you aren't losing it. You're just going to accidentally leave it behind. And if you're going to argue, will you please smile?" she urged. "I don't want Josh to think we're up to something."

"No," Marsha agreed with a wide and faintly sarcastic smile. "We mustn't let Josh know that we're plotting against him. If you want to leave a sweater behind for him to find, drop your own— and leave me out of it."

"Marsha, I can't. It would be too obvious if I left mine," Annette reasoned with forced calm. "It has to be yours so he won't get suspicious."

"And what happens if he doesn't see it? Or someone else sees it and steals it?" Marsha retorted. "Then I'm out a sweater."

"I'll buy you another one," Annette offered. "Will you do it?"

"Give me one good reason why I should," she challenged.

"Because you're my sister," Annette replied. "And I've helped you out of trouble a lot of times."

"You've also got me into it a lot of times," Marsha reminded her, then sighed. She wasn't even sure why she was resisting. She always gave in to Annette's mad plans, however reluctantly.

"Okay, I'll do it," she agreed, and added the warning, "But if I don't get my sweater back you're buying me a whole new tennis outfit, not just a sweater."

"That's a deal." Annette beamed her agreement to the terms, her gray eyes sparkling like burnished silver. "Let's go."

As they walked to the gate in the fence, she glanced at Josh. She was warmed by the discovery that he was watching her. It took all her control not to break into a smile. Instead, she lifted her head in an absent wave.

Josh acknowledged the salute with a nod of his head. When they started down the walk, Annette murmured instructions to her sister. "Let the sweater slide off your fingers while you pretend to be talking to me."

"What am I supposed to talk to you about?" Marsha asked anxiously. She had never been any good at subterfuge or deception.

"It doesn't matter." Annette tried not to let her exasperation creep out. "Just talk to me about what you can't think to talk about."

"I think I'm going to regret this," she murmured as she nervously tried to let go of the sweater so it could slide casually to the ground. "As a matter of fact, I know I am. I don't know how you always manage to talk me into these things. You'd think by now I'd have better sense, wouldn't you?"

The sweater was lying in the middle of the sidewalk. No one had called their attention to it, and

Annette breathed easier now that the mission was accomplished.

"You don't have anything to worry about," she soothed her sister's rattled nerves.

"What happens when he returns it? *If* he returns it?" Marsha questioned.

"I'll handle it," Annette promised. "You're going to be in the shower. I'll thank him for you, so there won't be any reason for you to even speak to him." She was well aware that one look at Marsha's guilty face and Josh would know it was a put-up job. He was going to guess it anyway, but she was going to see to it that he had plenty of reason to doubt his conclusion.

She glanced over her shoulder. They were already out of sight of the tennis courts. "Let's hurry," she urged her sister, and quickened her pace to a running walk.

"Why?"

"Because I want to be out of the shower before Josh comes," Annette answered, and broke into a run.

HER HANDS WERE TREMBLING as she twisted her hair into a demure knot on top of her head. Annette was certain she hadn't been this nervous on her first date. She had butterflies in her stomach and her knees were shaking. She secured her hair with a bobby pin and stepped back to view her overall reflection in the mirror.

"How do I look?" she asked Marsha, nervously moistening her dry lips.

The culotte-styled lounging robe was made out of dotted swiss fabric in a cool lime green. Its vee neckline had a single row of stand-up ruffles, which accented the slender curve of her neck. A white cinch belt nipped around her slender waist. With her blond hair swept atop her head in the little-girl knot and the clearness of her round gray eyes, she looked the picture of innocence.

"Like an angel," Marsha admitted in all truth.

Annette jumped when she heard the knock on the door. She breathed in deeply and looked at her sister for the reassurance of her moral support. "Go get in the shower," she ordered quickly. "And don't come out until I call you."

"Don't worry. I won't," Marsha promised, and scurried off to the bathroom.

Annette's legs felt like rubber as she walked to the door. The security chain was on it and she left it in place, opening the door a crack to peer outside. Josh had an arm braced against the door frame, still in his tennis clothes. His dark eyes gleamed with a mocking smile, but the line of his mouth was straight.

"Hello." Annette tried to sound surprised to see him, but her voice wasn't behaving very well.

"Hello," he returned the greeting in his well-modulated voice. He didn't alter his casually relaxed stance, silently waiting for her to open the door.

"Just a minute." She closed it to unhook the safety chain, then opened it.

Her heart was beating a rapid tattoo against

her ribs as she moved into the opening, blocked from stepping too far outside by his masculine bulk. The dark mahogany of his hair was attractively rumpled, its thickness inviting a smoothing hand. His gaze roamed leisurely over her, taking in every facet of her appearance and making it even more difficult for her to breathe normally.

"You need a sprig of lilies of the valley," Josh stated dryly.

"Oh?" Annette wondered if she sounded as disturbed as she felt.

"Yes. To go with those big gray eyes and that button nose," he explained. "With your hair like that, you look like a little girl on her way to Sunday school." His tone seemed to deride her youthfulness.

"I just got out of the shower." Annette touched a hand to her hair, wishing for a brief instant that she looked older. The thought was banished when she caught the glimpse of something smoldering in his eyes, especially when their glance swept over her as if probing beneath the robe to discover what she had on underneath.

"Yes, I noticed how fresh and clean you smell." Josh didn't appear too happy about making the admission, Annette noticed.

She was very conscious of his unique scent drifting about her, so male and stimulating to her senses. Her glance strayed to the breadth of his chest, the knit shirt clinging to its sinewy wall and stretching across the bunched muscles of his shoulders. The arm braced against the door frame was very near to her. She could see the sun-bleached hairs on his arm and wondered if they would be as silky to the touch as they looked. She shifted her gaze to his strong male features, but that didn't ease the turmoil his nearness aroused within her.

"Did you want something?" Annette asked in a surprisingly steady voice. His glance fell to her lips, and her heart stopped beating for a full second. Then his mouth tightened and the moment passed.

"You left this by the tennis courts." He lifted his other hand to show her the sweater and the room key between his fingers.

"I did?" She took it from him, her fingers tingling when they brushed against him.

"I admit it's a bit more subtle than a dropped handkerchief," Josh mocked the ploy to get him there. "A new twist on an old trick."

Annette pretended to examine the sweater. "Except that I didn't drop it," she replied. "This belongs to my sister, Marsha." She showed him the label inside the collar and the initial M stamped on the tag. "She must have left it."

When she lifted her gaze she saw the flicker of uncertainty in his eyes. Her plan was working. Josh couldn't be sure the sweater had been left deliberately.

"It's lucky you returned it. Marsha is in the shower," Annette explained, drawing his attention to the sound of running water coming from inside the hotel room, ''or she'd thank you herself. She didn't even miss it.''

''Then it isn't yours?'' Josh was still skeptical.

''It looks a lot like mine,'' she admitted. ''That's why I was confused when you first handed it to me. But mine has black trim to go with my tennis outfit. This is navy blue, so it's easy to mistake them.''

''Yes, it is.'' Josh continued to watch her closely.

It took all of Annette's skill to keep from betraying herself. ''If I hadn't had my room key with me, we probably would have noticed Marsha's sweater was missing and gone back to look for it. As it is, the key told you where to return it.''

''It was certainly convenient to find it in the sweater pocket,'' Josh agreed with a continuing trace of suspicion.

''Marsha's lucky it wasn't stolen. I don't know how to thank you. Maybe I should offer you a reward...or something....'' Her voice trailed off at the last, affected by the crooked slant of his hard masculine mouth.

''Or something,'' Josh murmured to indicate his choice was the latter.

A heady sexual tension enveloped Annette as his hand came up to lightly hold her chin, the touch of his fingers warm and firm. A tiny quiver ran through her at the contact. Josh leaned toward her, slowly bridging the space between them while his knowing gaze held hers. She was incapable of movement.

Her lashes drifted shut when his mouth settled onto her lips, his warm breath fanning them an instant before he claimed them. It was a tasting kiss, without demands or passion, yet incredibly evocative. His mouth's easy mobility revealed his experience, but there was no attempt to take her into his arms, not even when her lips softened under his light possession to invite a more demonstrative show of his skills.

Josh released her lips as slowly as he had taken them, and lifted his head to study her. The hand under her chin became absently caressing, his fingers lightly stroking the feminine lines of her throat. She felt on the edge of a precipice, ready to jump if he asked her.

The corners of his mouth deepened in faint amusement. "That's what you wanted me to do, wasn't it?" Josh challenged.

It was, but for the life of her, Annette couldn't answer him. Her lips continued to tingle with the sensations left by his kiss. Some very elemental message was being transmitted between them. When his hand came away from her chin, the connection was broken. Josh straightened to sever completely all silent communication.

His gaze flicked past her into the shadowed hotel room. "You should tell your sister to keep better track of her things."

"I will," Annette promised, but Josh had already turned to leave. "Thank you," she called after him.

As his long unhurried strides carried him away,

Annette remained outside the door a minute longer to watch him leave. Then her glance was pulled down to the sweater clutched in her hands. The elation of triumph propelled her inside the hotel room. An airy jubilant laugh spilled from her throat as she waltzed across the room and hugged herself, her eyes sparkling and alive.

"It worked, Marsha!" she called, trying to make herself heard above the noise of the shower.

"What?" came the half-muffled reply.

"I said it worked!" Annette shouted.

"I can't hear you!" she yelled back.

"Turn off the water!" It was several seconds before the noise subsided and Marsha ducked her head outside the bathroom door.

"Has he gone?" she asked.

"Yes." Annette was smiling broadly. "It worked!"

"Good. Another minute and I would have turned into a prune," Marsha declared.

Annette stared at her dripping sister as Marsha wrapped a towel around herself. "You haven't been in the shower all this time?"

There was a blank look at the question. "You told me to stay there until you called."

"You idiot," Annette laughed. "I meant that you should stay in the bathroom."

"That isn't what you said," Marsha retorted.

"Well, you weren't supposed to take me literally." It was very hard not to smile.

"Did he bring back my sweater?" Marsha changed the subject.

Annette presented it to her with a little flourish. "Here it is." Then she couldn't contain her excitement any longer. "He kissed me, Marsha."

"And?" Marsha thought surely there was an invitation to go out on a date. She would have thought that the dropped-sweater trick was worth more than a kiss.

"That's all," Annette admitted, but it didn't lessen the warm glow. "It's enough for now."

CHAPTER FOUR

THE ANGLING LIGHT from the morning sun glinted on the blue waters separating Wrightsville Beach from the mainland. Diving from overhead, a screeching gull swooped close to shore. Annette slowed out of her jogging trot into a walk, stretching her legs now and then so the muscles wouldn't cramp. She angled off the path onto the sandy beach. The small marina belonging to the hotel complex was in sight just ahead.

It had been another fruitless morning with no sign of Josh. She would have quit jogging every day except that she didn't want Josh to think that she ran only in the hopes of seeing him. She wanted him to believe it was part of her normal routine. Actually she was beginning to enjoy it and was physically invigorated by the exercise.

A chunk of blond hair had worked free of its ponytail. Annette slipped the elastic band off her hair and shook her head to let her hair tumble loose about her shoulders. Running her fingers through it, she lifted its long mass to let the cool sea breeze reach her scalp. Across the waters the mainland of North Carolina stood sharply against the horizon, and she paused to look at it.

Behind her she heard the sound of feet running through the sand toward her. She half turned to glance idly behind her. It was a full second before it registered that the young man with the burnished gold hair was Craig, the waiter. Without the uniform he looked very much the beach type in his pale blue slacks and the fishnet T-shirt in a darker shade of blue.

"Hello." His smile was wide and full of charm. "I knew if I kept looking I'd find you out here somewhere, jogging away the morning."

"You were right," Annette agreed with only a polite amount of welcome in her voice. He wasn't exactly the person she wanted to meet this morning, but when she resumed her walk, Craig fell in step beside her. "I take it you have the weekend off, or at least today," she remarked with a pointed glance at his clothes.

"The hotel rotates our schedules so everybody gets at least one full weekend off a summer. This is my turn," he explained. "Otherwise we just get an odd Saturday or Sunday off each month."

"I see," she murmured, not really interested.

He draped an arm familiarly around her shoulders, paying no attention to her start of surprise. Annette started to shrug it away, but she doubted that Craig would get the message. She continued to walk, indifferent to the arm around her shoulders.

"A buddy of mine is letting me have his day sailer for the weekend," he said, his head turned toward her as they trudged through the sand.

"It's going to be a perfect day for sailing. Why don't you come with me?"

Annette supposed that he expected her to fall all over herself in eagerness to accept his last-minute invitation. "Sorry." The smile was only a movement of her mouth as she signaled her refusal. "My family has already made plans for the day."

"So?" He didn't see where that was an obstacle. "You're a big girl now. You don't have to go with them."

Annette stopped and turned to face him, tipping her head back to look at him squarely so there could be no mistake that she meant what she said. The movement slipped his hand to only one shoulder.

"I don't have to go with them, but I want to," she stated.

"Come on," Craig cajoled. "You know you'll have more fun with me." When she didn't appear to be impressed he came up with his own reason why she wasn't. "I would have asked you yesterday but you weren't anywhere around."

"I doubt if it would have made any difference, Craig," Annette replied, trying to be as firm as she could without being rude. "I have fun being with my family."

"Yeah, but you can go with them anytime," he argued with a coaxing smile. "This is my only free time and I want you to spend it with me."

"I'm sorry, Craig," Annette patiently repeated her refusal.

He was too conceited to believe that she meant it, convinced that she only wanted to be persuaded. He tangled his hand in her hair. Annette didn't have a chance to do more than grab at his arm in protest before his mouth was crushing itself onto hers. She was not aroused by his hungry demand for a response to the kiss and was glad when he abruptly broke it off before she had to resort to more forcible resistance. He cast an anxious glance toward the hotel's marina, then let her go to step back.

His slightly guilty behavior aroused her curiosity, and Annette glanced in the same direction. A young girl, a member of the hotel staff, was sitting on the counter of a wood shelter on the dock where the hotel rented pedal boats and day sailers to their guests. The girl was looking in their direction.

"One of your girl friends?" Annette mocked him.

"Phyllis? No." He shook his head in an easy denial.

Annette made another guess. "I suppose the hotel has a policy against employees' fraternizing with the guests."

"Yeah," he admitted, but his smile indicated that he considered it a rule meant to be broken. "They aren't strict about it, though."

But he didn't repeat his invitation and Annette didn't bring it up. Her gaze went back to the marina, drawn to the two larger boats tied to the outer dock. The nearest one was about a fifty footer and the other was a few feet shorter.

"Does the hotel own those large boats tied up there, too?" she asked.

"Just the smaller one. The hotel charters it to small parties of guests for either fishing or harbor cruises," Craig informed her. "During the winter a lot of people come here for the sport fishing. When a person hooks into a marlin it's really a sight to see."

"I'll bet it is," Annette agreed. "What about the other boat?"

"That's Joshua Lord's new toy." Craig shifted, showing a discomfort with that subject. Annette tried not to reveal her suddenly increased interest in the boat. "I hadn't better hang around any longer or they'll put me to work," he joked, and regarded her intently. "Are you sure you won't change your mind and come with me today?"

"No, thanks." She shook her head to reinforce the refusal.

"It's your loss," he said to remind her that she was depriving herself of his company. "We could have had a ball." The corners of her mouth twitched with amusement as Craig backed away to leave. "I'll see you around." With a saluting wave he trotted off in the direction he'd come.

Laughing silently to herself at his incredible conceit, Annette started off, drawn toward the marina. She walked onto the dock for a closer look at Josh's impressive "toy." As she passed the girl on duty, Annette smiled a silent greeting. Then her gaze skipped over to the boat, recognizing the sleek lines of a Hatteras.

She had just walked past the bowlines when the girl at the marina called to her, "Hey, miss! That end of the dock is private!"

Annette turned around to explain, "I was just looking—"

But she was interrupted by the familiar timbre of Josh's voice. "It's all right, Chris," he told the girl. "She can pass."

Pivoting, Annette saw him standing on the aft deck of the boat. A pair of faded denims hugged his hips, riding low on his waist. The print shirt he was wearing was unbuttoned and hanging loose. There was a latent sexiness about him that curled around her and pulled her forward.

"Good morning." Annette paused by the gangplank. "I was just admiring your boat."

"Come aboard," Josh invited with a lazy look. "I'll give you a tour of her."

"I'd like that," she said, accepting the invitation and starting across, placing her hand in the one he offered to steady her.

His hand retained its hold on hers for a full second after she was standing on the deck beside him. He looked down at her steadily, a half smile on his mouth.

"I imagine your waiter friend told you who I am," he said.

The remark caused Annette to glance back along the beach where she had met Craig. She suddenly wondered whether Craig had broken off the meeting because of the girl or because of Josh. It was obvious that Josh had seen them together, so it was possible Craig had seen Josh and become worried about the security of his job.

"He did," she admitted, turning back to Josh and noticing his gaze drift to her mouth as if seeking a trace of Craig's stolen kiss. "But only in broad terms. He didn't get too specific." Annette hesitated, just a little unnerved by the almost physical quality of his glance. "Was there a reason why you didn't tell me you owned this resort—among other properties? Is it supposed to be a dark secret?"

"No." His smile deepened lazily. "I guess I expected our acquaintance to have a short duration, which made the information nonessential. But—" the challenging glitter in his gaze mocked her "—we seem to keep running into each other."

"We do, don't we?" Annette murmured, aware that she was stretching it too much to blame it on coincidence, so she didn't try. "Craig mentioned the boat was your new toy. She's a real beauty."

"Yes." It was a somewhat clipped agreement as Josh turned. "Let's go below and I'll show you the living quarters." He led the way down the steps. "Mind your head," Josh said, warning her of the low clearance that he had to duck but she didn't.

There was a subtle lushness about the quarters, hinted at by furniture covered in genuine leather and a solid mahogany bar cabinet. Annette looked around at the rich appointments, her feet sinking into a thick blue carpet.

"The crew's quarters are in the forward section." Josh indicated the door leading to them with a brief wave of his hand. He moved aft. "Here's the galley." It gleamed with all sorts of modern appliances.

Annette followed him down the companionway, past the head and the guest staterooms to the master stateroom. Her fingers brushed across the brown velvet cover on the oversize bed. "Like it?" Josh inquired.

"Yes," she nodded. "I'm very impressed." She was a little self-conscious standing next to the bed with Josh watching her. She didn't mean it to look like an invitation.

"I planned on taking her out for a short test run this morning," he said. "I'll probably be gone about an hour. Would you like to come along?"

"Yes," Annette accepted without any hesitation.

"Good." He smiled briefly. "You cast off the lines while I start the engines."

"Now I know why you asked me along." Annette grinned and followed him up the steps onto the aft deck. "You needed a deckhand."

"That's right, so be quick about it," Josh laughed.

"Aye, aye, sir." She moved nimbly forward to release the bowline.

The engines sputtered and throbbed powerfully to life as Annette cast off the stern. Josh slid her a brief glance when she joined him by the wheel, where he stood, his feet spread slightly apart.

"All clear," she said brightly.

Josh acknowledged the information with a nod and began to expertly maneuver the large boat away from the dock. A full panel of sophisticated navigational equipment was in front of him as well as the engine throttles and gauges.

There were few boats in the bay, still a little too early in the morning for the weekend sailors. Josh pointed the boat toward the distant mouth of the bay, keeping it at a reduced speed.

"The swells will be running a little rough this morning when we reach the ocean. Are you a good sailor?" Josh asked.

"Yes," Annette assured him. "Fortunately my sister is the only one in our family who gets seasick—and airsick." She hopped onto the little perch next to the controls. "What would you have done if I'd told you I was a poor sailor?"

"Taken you back," he answered flatly. "I've got guests coming aboard this afternoon, so I don't want any bother."

"Guests, huh?" She felt a little twinge of jealousy. "Male or female?"

"Both." Josh arched his eyebrows in a knowing glance, as if reading her thoughts.

"A party. Sounds like fun," she lied.

"An adult party," he informed her, in case she intended to try to wangle an invitation.

She wrinkled her nose at him. "How boring!" His throaty chuckle warmed her in spite of her envy for those who would enjoy his company that afternoon. "Is your party part business or strictly pleasure?"

"No matter how they start out, they usually end up a combination of both," Josh replied, and stepped away from the controls. "I'm going up on the fly bridge. Want to come?"

Annette answered by following him to the open bridge aloft. A salty breeze whipped at her hair as she sat down on a front cushioned seat and curled her legs under her. Beyond the bridge ahead, she could see the first hint of breakers.

With the throb of the engines, the chatter on the marine radio and the rush of the surf, conversation was reduced to a minimum once they were at sea. It was the shortest hour Annette could remember, the marina coming into view all too soon to suit her. As Josh maneuvered the boat into dock, she started to leave the bridge.

"You don't need to bother, Annette," Josh called her back. "Fred will make her fast," he said, obviously referring to the man standing by on the dock.

She kept her seat while the boat was being secured. Once the engines were switched off it seemed unnaturally quiet. Standing, she faced him, wishing there was a way to prolong the moment.

"I wish we were just going out instead of coming back," Annette admitted frankly. "Thanks for letting me come along."

"It was my pleasure." Josh smiled distantly, watching her with a hooded look, his hands resting casually on his hips.

Unable to find an adequate reason to postpone taking her leave from him, Annette attempted a bright smile. "I hope you have fun at your party this afternoon."

"I'm sure I will," he replied. "You have fun on your date."

"Date?" She lifted her head in vague confusion.

His gaze narrowed. "Won't you be seeing Craig this afternoon?"

Annette hesitated and decided against denying it outright, catching a hint of jealousy in the expression on his taut features. "Isn't it against hotel policy for guests and employees to mingle?"

"Did Craig tell you that?" Josh mocked.

"Yes," she admitted.

"Before or after he kissed you?" he challenged with a trace of harshness.

"As a matter of fact, it was after. You saw it, did you?" she murmured, her gray eyes eagerly watching every nuance of his expression.

"When a couple kiss on a public beach, someone is likely to see them," he pointed out.

"I think Craig saw you," Annette surmised. "Which explains why he left so soon after that. He probably thought he'd get in trouble."

"I have a hunch that you spell trouble for just about every man who comes in contact with you," John said.

A faint smile touched her mouth. "Including you, Josh?"

"Yes, including me," he admitted dryly, an amused light gleaming in his dark eyes.

Her movement seemed to be idly directed, but it brought her a little closer to him. She tipped her head back slightly to regard him with curious speculation. Her pulse raced a little under his steady gaze.

"You strike me as the kind of man who never does anything he doesn't want to do. The other afternoon, when you kissed me...." Annette paused a second "Was it what you wanted to do?"

"You know damn well it was." There was a lazy curve to his mouth, as if he were silently laughing.

"I wasn't sure," she replied with a mild shrug, but a thread of excitement was running through her veins.

"Weren't you?" he challenged huskily.

Then his hand was under her chin, as it had been that afternoon, but it didn't stay there long. It slid along her neck to tunnel under her hair while it urged her toward him. Annette needed little persuasion, flowing naturally into his arms.

His mouth burned on hers, erasing any remaining trace of Craig's kiss. His possession bore no resemblance to the chaste kiss of the other afternoon. Josh allowed for no innocence as he plundered the softness of her lips, taking them with a sexual appetite that left her in no doubt of his hunger.

The heat of his body enveloped her completely with languid warmth. His roaming hands pressed her curves to the hard contours of his length, awakening her flesh to their differences and stimulating it. Annette was reeling from the upheaval his kiss was creating within her system. This rawly sensual embrace was shaking her to the core, disrupting her preconceived thoughts of what it should be like. It was all so shockingly new that she didn't know what she was thinking or feeling. Nothing was as she expected it to be.

When Josh dragged his mouth from her lips, it moistly grazed a path to her neck. Dazed into submission, she turned her head aside to allow him access to the quivering pulse in her throat. Her fingers were curled in the material of his shirt for support, her knees weak and trembling.

"I must be out of my mind," he muttered harshly against her skin. "You're just a child. You're not even of legal age yet."

"Would you feel better if I told you I have a birthday coming up in two days?" Annette whispered, afraid that he would stop whatever it was that he was doing to her—and afraid that he would continue.

"No, it wouldn't." His hands abruptly gripped her shoulders and held her away from him. A mixed anger blazed darkly in his eyes. "Didn't anybody teach you that it's dangerous to play with fire?"

"Yes." Her head moved in a small nod.

"Then you ought to know you can't always put it out when you want to," Josh stated grimly.

"I know," she admitted, not liking the way he was treating her like a child when, in fact, she wasn't one. At the moment, it was immaterial that he didn't know it.

"Do you?" he challenged. "To you, a kiss is one step beyond holding hands. But to me, it's one step away from the bed! That's where this one will lead, you know." His gaze narrowed on the warmth that flooded her cheeks. "No, you don't know, do you?"

"Josh, I—" Annette wanted to change the subject, suddenly unable to handle the topic of sex.

"You thought it would be exciting and a little dangerous to flirt with an older man," he accused roughly. "It made you feel a little wicked to tease me and tempt me with your little Lolita act."

"That isn't true!" she protested angrily, but Josh wasn't listening.

"I've outgrown doctor games. If you want to play 'touchy-feely,' go find your blond Adonis." He turned her away and aimed her toward the dock, propelling her forward by his hard grip above her elbow. "He's probably still in that stage."

His blazing anger only aroused hers. When he released her to adjust the gangplank so she could disembark, it burned her throat raw and stung her eyes with hot tears.

As Josh faced her again to escort her from the boat, Annette glared at him proudly. "I am not a child."

His features were drawn in a hard mask as his gaze bored into her, then swept past her to shore. "No? I have a hunch that's *daddy* looking this way," he murmured on a slightly sarcastic note.

Annette jerked her head around to look, instantly spying her father and Kathleen on the beach with Robby. There was no mistake that her father was looking their way with narrowing interest.

"If he knew what you were up to," Josh said, "he'd take you over his knee and spank you. Which is precisely what you need!"

"Maybe I'm into spankings!" Annette flashed, and turned to cross the gangplank to the dock, her carriage stiff with pride. But she didn't turn quickly enough to miss seeing the ridge of his jaw go white with anger.

There was a small degree of satisfaction in the. knowledge that he was infuriated. But all his references to her as a child continued to sting. She would enjoy sweet revenge when Josh found out how old she really was. In her anger, Annette didn't remember that age wasn't the only issue. There was still the matter of her sexual inexperience, which the number of her years didn't change.

As she walked off the dock onto the beach, Annette fought to secure her poise. At this juncture, she didn't want her father suspecting that anything unusual had happened aboard the boat. Like Josh, he wasn't an easy man to fool. She would need all her wits about her to keep his suspicions at bay.

Unable to postpone this meeting with her father, Annette inhaled calm steadying breaths and willed the constriction in her throat to ease. She blinked at the hot moisture in her eyes and struggled to appear cool and collected as she approached the family group.

"Well, good morning," Kathleen greeted her, as if nothing were amiss. "We missed you at breakfast."

"Would you help me build a sand castle, Annette?" Robby had dug a trench in the sand with his shovel, making the initial inroads for a moat. "Mom isn't very good at them."

"Thanks a lot, fella!" Kathleen laughed at the criticism.

"Sure. After a while, okay?" Annette promised her little brother, aware of shrewd gray eyes watching her closely.

"Where have you been, Annette?" her father asked quietly—too quietly for her raw nerves.

"Out." But she knew he wouldn't settle for that ambiguous and slightly sassy answer. "For a boat ride," she answered.

Robby looked up, disappointment crossing his face. "I want to go for a boat ride. Can I?" he asked. "Will you take me?"

"Later on we'll rent one of those pedal boats," Annette suggested in a futile attempt to distract the conversation. "Would you like that?"

"Boy! Yeah!" he agreed with wide-eyed enthusiasm.

But her father zeroed back in on the subject. "Who was that man on the boat with you? Do you know him?"

"Of course I know him," Annette laughed with pseudobrightness. "You don't think I'd go boat riding with a stranger, do you? He's Joshua Lord. He owns this hotel—as well as the boat."

"Oh." His mouth curved in a half-smile as his gray eyes gleamed with curious speculation. "When did you start traveling in such exalted circles?"

"Oh, dad, he's only a man, for heaven's sake," Annette protested.

"He's a little old for you, don't you think?" he replied.

She didn't have to fake the mocking laugh that came from her throat. "He said almost the same thing, dad, except that he turned it around and said I was too young. So I guess you have nothing to worry about." She lifted her shoulders in an expressive shrug and smiled. Jordan Long offered no comment. Mentally crossing her fingers, Annette hoped the subject was closed. "Where's Marsha?"

"I think she's still in bed sleeping," Kathleen replied. "We knocked at the door when we left our rooms, but she didn't answer."

"She's probably still asleep," Annette agreed. "She was up until after three o'clock last night— reading a book." She backed away a step, preparing to make her departure. "I'll go wake her up. We'll join you after we've eaten breakfast."

"We'll be here on the beach," Kathleen said.

As Annette walked away, Kathleen noticed how closely Jordan watched his oldest child.

There was a quietness about him that she wasn't used to seeing. She glanced at Annette's disappearing figure, then back to Jordan.

"Is something wrong, Jordan?" she asked.

He seemed to drag his gaze away from Annette before meeting her questioning eyes. That mouth she loved so well was twisted in a wryly grim line.

"Yes," he answered her question with a simple affirmative.

"What is it?" Kathleen wanted more of an answer than that. "Annette?"

"Yes. I didn't like that look in her eyes," he replied. "She's up to something." His glance strayed to the boat tied up at the dock. "I have a feeling that 'something' is Joshua Lord."

Kathleen remembered his comment that the man was too old for Annette and guessed the direction of Jordan's concern. "I wouldn't worry about Annette, Jordan. She's much too intelligent to be talked into anything." A quick smile crossed her mouth. "More than likely, Annette's talking him into something."

"One of these days she's going to meet her match, Kathleen," Jordan warned.

She sat back on her heels. "Chauvinist," she laughed. "I think you're actually hoping that she does. It bothers you when a woman outsmarts a man, doesn't it?"

"You come here and I'll show you what bothers me," he murmured in a suggestive mock threat.

Her breath caught in her throat as she started

to sway toward him. Then Robby reminded her of his presence.

"Mommy, will you help me? I can't make the walls of my castle stand up," he complained in a disheartened voice.

"You're the one with the engineering degree, Jordan," Kathleen smiled. "Help your son."

He started to move to comply with her request, then paused to tilt her chin up. "Wrong. It's *our* son—or have you forgotten it takes two?"

"Maybe you'll have to refresh my memory," Kathleen suggested huskily. "Later."

"You can count on it." He ran his thumb across her lips and moved away to help Robby.

LATER THAT AFTERNOON, Annette took Robby out on one of the pedal boats as she had promised. The bay was filled with families of afternoon sailors in boats of every size and description. She kept their foot-powered boat close to shore, away from the congestion.

When she saw Josh's boat maneuvering away from the dock, she couldn't help looking. As it drifted slowly by the little cove where she was, Annette saw his guests. One in particular caught her eye. A raven-haired witch in a scarlet swimsuit was draped all over Josh. Annette could well imagine the "business" that woman had in mind.

She was consumed with jealousy. If she'd been close enough she would have plucked out every black hair on the girl's head, one by one. She hadn't guessed she could feel such a rage—or such pain—at seeing Josh with another woman.

"Annette, you'd better look where we're going," Robby admonished. "You nearly ran over a duck."

She looked to the front and saw the bird taking wing. "Sorry," she murmured.

He looked at her. "Are you crying?"

"No, of course not!" she denied, and blinked at the wetness welling in her gray eyes.

CHAPTER FIVE

ANNETTE ROLLED the toothpick-speared olive around the martini glass, staring absently at the hypnotic circles. Her dress of silver chiffon swooped modestly low in the front, showing off the golden tan of her shoulders and arms. The salon's stylist had swept one side of her tawny hair away from her face, adding a touch of sophistication to her features. An artful application of makeup had enhanced the smoke gray of her eyes and the fullness of her dark lashes.

She was oblivious to her mature appearance, just as she was oblivious to the members of her family seated around the table in the hotel's dining room. There was talk and laughter, but Annette didn't hear any of it. They had gathered to celebrate her birthday, but she didn't feel much like celebrating anything.

"You've barely touched your martini, Annette." Her father's voice prodded her into an awareness of them. "Is it too dry?"

"No, it's fine," she assured him, and let go of the pick to take a sip of the drink.

"Do you want to taste my Shirley Temple?" Robby offered. "It's good."

"No, thanks." She smiled wanly. "You drink it."

"Does Annette have to wait until after dinner to open her gifts or can we give them to her now?" Marsha asked eagerly.

"That's up to Annette," Kathleen replied.

"It doesn't matter to me." Annette indicated her indifference with a slight lift of a shoulder. "Whatever you want to do."

"Then we'll give them to her now," Marsha said, deciding for the rest of them. She picked up the gift-wrapped box by her chair.

Jordan Long eyed Annette quietly. "I think everyone is more eager to give you presents than you are to receive them." He glanced at his wife and mocked, "Are you sure it's her birthday?"

"I'm sorry, dad." Annette realized she had to summon some enthusiasm for the party, regardless of her personal mood.

"Open mine first," Marsha urged.

Her smile was plastic as she took the box from her sister and began loosening the bright ribbon. Marsha's expression was alive with animation, her blue eyes sparkling like sapphires. Annette couldn't help thinking how beautiful Marsha was when she forgot to be self-conscious.

"It has to be clothes." Annette started the guessing game their family always played while opening presents. "I'll bet you bought me something blue—so you can borrow it."

"Wait and see," Marsha laughed.

When she lifted the lid, Annette discovered she

had been half-right. A soft summer lilac slacks-and-top set was hidden in folds of tissue. "It's beautiful," she said, assuring Marsha that she liked the gift, and added a laughing, "And it isn't blue."

"Now it's my turn," Robby insisted. "Open mine!"

Sensitive to his fragile child's ego, Annette went through the full wide-eyed pretense of guessing what was inside the paper-flat package. Robby was giggling wildly at her absurd guesses. He'd drawn her a picture of Wrightsville Beach, complete with the two of them in a pedal boat. Not that Annette recognized either of the stick figures, but Robby pointed them out and identified them for her.

"I'll hang it up on my bedroom wall when we get home," she promised. "We'll make a frame and everything for it." And Robby was certain he had given her the most prized gift of all. He couldn't know the scene contained bittersweet memories.

"Here." Her father placed a small gift-wrapped box in front of her. "This is from Kathleen and me."

"I can hardly wait until you open it," Marsha murmured anxiously.

"Do you know what it is?" Annette asked.

"Yes. Daddy showed it to me," her sister admitted.

"Something this small has to mean jewelry." She glanced at her father, then Kathleen. Both watched her. "It can't be a watch. You gave me one for graduation."

When she snapped open the jeweler's case, Annette didn't have to pretend surprise or delight. Her response was genuine as she gazed at the diamond stud earrings inside. She looked at her father.

"Are they real?" she whispered.

"If they aren't, they are very expensive imitations," he declared.

There was a small lump in her throat when she glanced at her stepmother. "It was your idea, wasn't it, Kathleen?" Annette stated with a knowing smile, and felt the comfortable encirclement of family love. "I'm glad we picked you for a mother."

"Now wait a minute, Annette." Her father reached out to curl his fingers possessively around the hand Kathleen rested on the table. "I know you like to take credit for finding Kathleen, but I ultimately did the picking."

"Dad, you're just like all men," Annette declared with a faint sparkle in her eyes. "You have to be prodded once in a while."

"Is that a fact?" He eyed her with amused tolerance.

"It is," she stated. "A woman has to put ideas in a man's head. There might have been only four of us sitting at this table tonight if Marsha and I hadn't put in a request for a brother."

"As I recall, I was thinking about little boys

long before you mentioned that," her father chuckled.

As Annette removed one earring from its velvet bed, Marsha volunteered, "Let me help you put them on."

With her sister's assistance she didn't need a mirror, but she wished for one. "How do they look?" She had to rely on her family to admire the results.

"Fantastic!" Marsha assured her, and the others added similar praise.

Pushing out of her chair, Annette walked around the table to her parents. "Thank you, daddy." She bent down and kissed his cheek, then turned and hugged Kathleen. "Thank you both."

When she straightened and turned to walk back to her chair, Annette found herself face to face with Josh. For a heart-stopping second the smile on her lips froze in place as she stared into his enigmatic brown eyes. Tension seared the air between them, heating her blood. It thawed her expression, as she was unable to deny the raw pleasure that seeing him gave.

Her gaze wandered over his handsomely hewed features and lingered an instant on the strong line of his mouth, remembering how his kisses had destroyed her preconceived notions of love's feelings at their last meeting. She became conscious that he was dressed in a dark evening suit and tie, his white shirt contrasting sharply with his sun-browned skin. The formal attire gave him a worldly air, a male urbanity that excited and challenged.

All the while Annette had been observing the changes in him, Josh had been noticing her sophisticated appearance. He took special note of her hairstyle, dress and makeup. When his inspection was concluded, cynicism flickered in his expression and Annette realized he considered her appearance to be an adolescent's version of dress-up.

She was reminded of her parting declaration to him two days earlier that she wasn't a child. Fate was offering her a ready-made opportunity to prove it.

There are occasions when time has a way of appearing to stand still. Although it seemed they had looked at each other for long minutes, in fact, only seconds had passed.

"Good evening, Annette." Josh broke the silence initially.

"Good evening." She nodded demurely, poise sweeping through her with remarkable strength. The moment of pleasant revenge was at hand and she didn't intend to let it escape. "I'd like you to meet my family, Mr. Lord."

A dark eyebrow arched briefly at the formal term of address, cool amusement glinting in his eyes. Then Josh was dragging his gaze from her and turning to speak to someone else.

"I'll join you in a few minutes," he said, drawing Annette's attention to the two middle-aged men in business suits standing patiently beside him, while the restaurant hostess hovered close by to show them to their table.

Before that moment she hadn't been aware anyone was with him. It staggered her to discover she could be so unobservant, but Josh's presence had a way of blinding her to everything else. There was a murmur of acceptance from the two men as they moved away to follow the hostess.

With a graceful turn, Annette included her family in her meeting with Josh. Courteously her father stood up as she began the introductions, beginning with him.

"Dad, I'd like you to meet Joshua Lord." Then she reversed it. "Mr. Lord, this is my father, Jordan Long."

The two men shook hands, exchanging polite phrases. Her father was unusually reserved, his gray eyes sharp in their inspection of Josh, measuring him without revealing his ultimate conclusion. That in itself warned Annette that her father was not favorably impressed with Josh. It made her a little uneasy.

She continued the round of introductions, progressing from Kathleen to Marsha and concluding with Robby. It was her little brother who introduced, in his ingenuous way, the information she wanted Josh to learn.

"Are you here for Annette's birthday party?" Robby wanted to know. "Did you bring her a present?" He didn't wait for an answer. "Show him what I made you, Annette."

The line of Josh's mouth was half-curved in a

smile when his dark gaze met hers. It slid to the table and the abandoned gift wrappings at her place setting.

"You did mention you had a birthday coming up," Josh remembered. "I didn't realize it was today. When you're young, it's a cause for celebration. Happy birthday, Annette."

"Thank you." Inwardly she raged at his reference to her being young, but she concealed it, except for a brief silvery flare of temper in her eyes.

"Show him what I gave you," Robbie repeated his request, paying no attention to Kathleen's attempts to hush him.

"Robby drew me a picture." Annette reached across the table to pick up the drawing, motivated by her own self-interest to keep the subject of her birthday alive.

"It's very good." Josh obligingly admired it.

"She's going to hang it on her wall when we get home," Robby informed him proudly.

"Robby, can you tell Mr. Lord how old I am today?" Annette asked, and slid a complacently mocking glance at Josh.

"She's twenty years old," her little brother readily supplied the information. Josh studied her with a sharply narrowed look. "I can count to twenty," Robby declared. "Do you want me to count it for you?"

Annette held Josh's gaze, partially screening it with her lashes. "Out of the mouths of babes," she murmured for his ears alone.

While Marsha was convincing Robby that it

wasn't necessary for him to count all the way to twenty, a mixture of reactions ran across Josh's features—skepticism, shock, irritation and a glittering kind of amusement that promised to get even.

"So you're twenty years old," Josh murmured.

"It's hard to believe, isn't it?" she smoothly taunted him.

His mouth twisted dryly. "I guess daddy's little girl has grown up."

"In some people's eyes, we always remain little girls." Annette was subtly asking whether Josh still regarded her in that light.

Her father inserted an agreement with that opinion, simultaneously confirming her age. "Ten or twenty, Annette will always be my little girl."

"Since I'm not in your position," Josh told her father, indirectly responding to Annette's subtle question, "it makes a difference."

Her father's gaze narrowed in veiled suspicion, sensing some silent message had been passed. "It was a pleasure meeting you, Mr. Lord, but we shouldn't keep you from your guests any longer."

It was easy for Annette to read between the lines of her father's polite words. Josh was being invited to leave. She didn't offer any objections, her purpose achieved. Josh appeared to take the dismissal well, although his eyes mocked her slightly because her father was still vetting the men in her life.

"Happy birthday, Annette," Josh repeated, then moved away to rejoin his party.

From her chair, Annette had a clear view of the table where Josh was seated at right angles to her. She could observe him all evening without half trying.

"Is that man your boyfriend?" Robby asked.

"I wouldn't exactly call him that, no," Annette replied, aware of her father's studied look. "He's a man friend."

"It's getting late." Kathleen deftly altered the subject, which she realized was a sensitive issue to her husband, by reminding him that Robby's bedtime was quickly approaching. "Perhaps we should order."

"Yes, of course," he agreed absently, and signaled the waiter to bring menus to the table.

While the waiter was passing the menus around, the wine steward approached the table with a wine bucket and stand—and an iced magnum of champagne. He set it next to Annette's chair. Her father's gaze narrowed on it with displeasure.

"We didn't order that," he informed the steward.

"No, sir," the man agreed, and expertly popped the cork. "It's compliments of Mr. Lord." With a towel wrapped around the bottle, he splashed some in a glass for Annette. "Madam?" It was a veiled request for her approval.

As she looked across the dining room to Josh's

table, she lifted the glass to her mouth. Josh was watching her, their eyes meeting across the distance. Annette held the glass close to her lips, not immediately sipping the champagne as she inhaled its heady bouquet and let the bubbles tickle her nose.

Josh raised his drink in a silent toast to her. When he took a drink of it, Annette quivered with the disturbing sensation that he was drinking the essence of her. A little shaken, she lowered her gaze and sipped at the champagne, its alcoholic effervescence tingling down her throat.

"It's very good," she commented, assuring the steward of the champagne's excellence.

After he filled her glass, the steward poured champagne for the others. Robby fussed because he didn't get any, but Kathleen distracted him with the menu, helping him choose his evening meal.

"You're looking quite pleased with yourself, Annette," her father remarked with narrowed interest.

"It's my birthday," she reminded him, as if that were the reason.

But he wasn't buying it. "That didn't seem to matter earlier."

"That was before I opened my presents," Annette countered.

"That was also before Joshua Lord stopped by the table," he murmured.

"Daddy, you sound just like a father," she chided.

The waiter returned to take their order, and Annette was relieved to have the conversation changed. Her father remained quiet throughout the meal, but he didn't mention Joshua Lord again. He was never out of Annette's mind, however, or her sight. And more than once, Josh looked in her direction, which only added to the soft glow about her.

When it came time to leave, the magnum of champagne was still more than half-full. "Would madam like to take it with her?" the steward inquired with exaggerated formality.

"Please," Annette answered with a nod.

"What are you going to do with that?" her father questioned with veiled sharpness.

"Take it back to the room and celebrate my birthday," she answered him with breezy innocence. "The night is young. Who knows how late Marsha and I will stay up?"

He didn't look completely pleased or satisfied with her explanation, but he didn't belabor the point. With the addition of the champagne bottle to her other presents, Annette accepted her sister's offer to help carry some of them. As the family left the table, Annette smiled across the room to Josh. There was a responding movement of his mouth and something else in his look that Annette was certain she interpreted correctly.

At the hotel room she shared with Marsha, she and her sister parted company from her parents and Robby as they continued to their own suite of rooms around the corner. Inside the room, Marsha laid her present to Annette on the dresser.

"Why don't you try your new outfit on and see how it fits?" Marsha suggested.

"I'll wait till tomorrow," Annette replied absently, preoccupied with other plans. She stopped in front of the mirror and inspected her reflection, using her fingers to touch up her hairstyle.

Marsha paused curiously to watch. "Are you really going to drink that champagne tonight?"

"Part of it." Annette opened her silver evening purse and took out the tube of lipstick. Uncapping it, she twisted the stick up and began outlining her lips with its dusky rose color.

"What are you doing?" Marsha frowned.

"Putting on lipstick. What does it look like I'm doing?" She blotted it with a tissue.

"Why?" Which is what Marsha had meant initially.

"Why do you think?" Annette countered, and picked up the champagne bottle and a glass the hotel supplied to the rooms.

"Are you going out?" Marsha stared, already guessing the answer was affirmative but asking it anyway. "Where?"

"To meet Josh, of course." Annette started toward the door, the chiffon skirt swishing about her shapely legs.

"But...how...? When...?" Marsha faltered over the questions, unable to complete any of them.

"There wasn't any arrangement made for us to meet." She guessed the cause of her sister's confusion. "But he'll be waiting for me just the same." With a Cheshire smile on her face, she turned to wink at Marsha. "Don't wait up for me."

She was sweeping out the door before Marsha could recover enough to question how Annette knew Josh would be there. This time she was really worried about the kind of trouble her sister was getting involved in. She was playing in the adult leagues now, and the consequences could be serious.

WITH ROBBY TUCKED IN for the night, Kathleen moved quietly out of her son's darkened room and into the larger adjoining room where she and Jordan slept. He was standing at the window, looking out into the night. His suit jacket and tie were thrown across the bed. Kathleen started to go hang them up, but something in his brooding stance pulled her to Jordan instead.

Approaching from behind, she slid her arms around his middle and felt him stiffen an instant in surprise at her touch, then relax. She laid her cheek against his back, enjoying the warmth of his body.

"A penny for your thoughts?" she murmured.

He stirred restlessly. She loosened her encircling arms as he turned away from the window to face her. His glance touched her, cynically gray and thoughtful.

"I have a feeling Joshua Lord is worth a lot more than a penny," Jordan replied dryly, and curved an arm around her shoulders to hug her to his side.

Kathleen smoothed a hand across his shirt-front, feeling the hard muscles of his chest beneath the material. It was a pleasant intimacy to touch him like this—to have the freedom of loving him.

"He's probably worth two pennies at least," Kathleen agreed on a playful note. Her expression became absently thoughtful as she remembered the meeting. "He's a very attractive man."

A finger was hooked under her chin to tilt her head up for Jordan's bemused study. "You thought so, did you?" he accused lightly.

"Yes," she admitted calmly, and a light danced amid the olive flecks in her hazel eyes. "Jealous?"

"Should I be?" he asked, but he wasn't really serious.

"No." Kathleen had no desire to let him wonder. Their time together was too precious to waste it playing games when they could be loving.

As if hearing her silent thoughts, Jordan kissed her warmly yet briefly, betraying that his mind was still concentrating on something else. His caressing hand wound its fingers into her auburn hair and pressed her head against his shoulder. Bending his head slightly, he rubbed his jaw against her hair.

"Annette was certainly in a better mood after she saw him," he remarked with seeming idleness.

"She seemed to be," Kathleen agreed.

"Has she said anything to you about this Lord character?" For all his attempt to be casual, there was a stiffness in his words,

"No." Kathleen half smiled but was careful not to let Jordan see it—or suspect.

"What do you suppose is going on between them?" he asked.

"Assuming, of course, that something is going on between them," Kathleen said, reminding him that they didn't know whether there was or not. "Annette said something the other day that Joshua Lord considered her to be too young."

"That was a red herring." Jordan dismissed it as having no significance. "Their age difference isn't any greater than ours."

"I suppose not," she agreed. "Then what bothers you? I'm not sure that I understand."

"Didn't you see the way he looked at her?" he demanded. "He wants her. I saw it in his eyes."

Her chin quivered with her effort to hold back the laughter, but she failed. It spilled softly from her throat. There was irritation in the grip of his hands as he held her away from him. His challenging look indicated he was anything but amused by her reaction.

"Did I say something funny?" He insisted on an explanation.

"I'm sorry, but you sounded so righteous." She really tried to contain her amusement, but it danced in her eyes. "What do you think was in your eyes when you looked at me?"

"That's different," Jordan replied impatiently.

The dimples in her cheeks deepened with her effort to hide her silent laughter. "Naturally," she murmured. "Annette is your daughter—which makes all the difference in the world."

For an instant he looked angry, then amused chagrin stole over his expression. "I sounded very fatherly, didn't I?"

"Yes, you did," Kathleen smiled widely.

"I can't help worrying that he's too experienced for her," he explained.

"I wouldn't worry about it if I were you. It's probably just a holiday romance." Kathleen shrugged her lack of concern. "We've been here—what—two weeks? And we'll be leaving in another couple of weeks. What can happen in a month's time?"

"If you are trying to reassure me, you just failed," Jordan smiled. "Or have you forgotten that we fell in love in less than a month?"

"Remind me," she invited, and Jordan gathered her into his arms.

CHAPTER SIX

THE MOONLIGHT SHIMMERED on the glassy surface of the Atlantic Ocean while the night-lights of Wrightsville Beach faded the stars in the sky. The air was fresh and soft, washed clean by the sea breezes of the Atlantic. The languid warmth of the day clung to the night.

On the curving edge of the beach, Annette paused and balanced on one foot to slip off a high-heeled sandal, then shifted her position to remove the other. With the champagne bottle in one hand and her shoes and glass in the other, she wandered onto the beach in her nylon-stockinged feet. The fine grains of sand were cool beneath her toes when she stopped short of the tidemark to gaze at the calm waters of the sea.

The unhurried sound of strolling footsteps broke the stillness of the night. Turning from the waist up, Annette looked back toward the hotel. A warm run of pleasure raced through her when she recognized the shadowed male figure as Josh. His stride didn't change as he angled across the sand to her.

A little more than a foot away, he stopped. There was a serenity about his expression, but a disturbing light burned in his eyes. Without the advantage of the added height her high-heeled sandals gave her, Annette had to tip her head back to gaze into his eyes.

"I knew you'd be here." His voice was quietly strong.

"I knew you'd come," Annette replied.

Neither of them found it necessary to explain the source of their knowledge, some primitive recess of their minds that was purely instinct. It was enough that they had both listened to it.

"Would you like some champagne?" She indicated the bottle with a lifting gesture of her hand. "I only brought one glass so we'll have to share. Do you mind?"

"No."

Josh took the bottle from her and worked the cork out with his thumbs. It made a small popping sound when it came free. Annette held out the glass for him to fill, her shoes dangling from a finger by their heel straps.

"Ladies first," Josh said, indicating he would wait to drink after her.

Annette transferred the glass to her other hand and carried it to her lips, sipping the now tepid wine while she continued to regard him. A heady excitement licked through her veins, but it had nothing to do with the alcoholic content of the champagne.

He watched her drink, his lazily sensuous gaze taking note of her shining lips pursed to the rim of the glass. It tracked the liquid down her throat as she swallowed and it stopped in the vicinity of her breasts. Annette quivered inwardly with the sensation that Josh could see through the chiffon material covering them. The impression was lost when he lifted his gaze back to her face.

"Here." She offered him the glass when she was through, and it was her turn to watch him.

If either of them noticed the champagne had gone flat, they didn't mention it. Her senses were alive to his presence, the sheen of the moonlight on his tanned features, the masculine fragrance of his cologne, the penetrating study of his gaze and the even sound of his breathing.

"It's a beautiful night, isn't it?" she commented as he refilled the glass and handed it to her.

"Perfect," Josh agreed.

"Yes." Her voice was a little breathless. "Champagne, moonlight and. . . a little romance. What better way for a girl to celebrate her twentieth birthday?"

The question was a softly provocative challenge to remind him of his mistaken impression of her age. The corners of his mouth deepened with amusement.

"Why didn't you tell me how old you were?" he countered with a challenge of his own.

"Would you have believed me? You were convinced I was seventeen," Annette reminded him, and lowered her gaze to the glass of champagne. "Besides, you might have been the kind of man who gets turned on by sweet young things."

" 'Sugar and spice and everything nice,' " Josh quoted. "There is definitely more spice in your makeup."

"Do your tastes run to spicy things?" she asked.

"I can't imagine anything more boring than a bland diet," he replied.

"Neither can I," Annette agreed. "I hope you realize how frustrating it was trying to act the age you thought I was."

"I hope you realize how frustrating it was trying to treat you like the girl I thought you were instead of the woman I wanted you to be," Josh countered. "You knew that. And you deliberately provoked me."

"Why, Mr. Lord, whatever do you mean?" Impish lights danced in her innocently rounded gray eyes.

"You can drop the prim and proper act," he advised with a mocking slant to his mouth. "I'm wise to you now."

"Are you?" she murmured, and carried the glass to her mouth for another sip of the champagne.

"Yes. And you've had enough of that." Josh took the glass from her hand and emptied its contents into the sand. Then he tossed it and the bottle onto the beach.

"You shouldn't litter," Annette admonished, anticipation of his intentions rushing along her nerve ends.

"We'll pick them up—later," he said, and

reached for her shoes to rid her hands of them, too. They made a soft little plop as they landed on the sand.

When Josh faced her again, neither was holding anything. "You've enjoyed the moonlight and drunk champagne. Now it's time for some of that romance you mentioned earlier."

His hands spanned her slender waist to draw her to him. It seemed to Annette that she floated into his arms. It was all so unhurried. Confidence seared her. It was happening just the way she had planned it.

"I was beginning to wonder whether you heard me say that," she murmured when his face was very close to hers.

His warm breath caressed her lips as his mouth hovered above them. "I heard you."

Nothing was held back when Josh kissed her, not his experience and not his desire. Annette was engulfed by a force more potent than she realized. It fired her senses and melted her body to his solidly muscled flesh. Her mouth was filled with the taste of him. It induced a languor more dangerous than any from champagne.

The wild rhythm in her ears was the drumming of her heartbeat, gloriously loud and primitive. Roaming male hands applied pressure, arching her spine to fit her more intimately to his body. Her fingers combed themselves into his hair, its texture vital and thick.

His nibbling mouth teased an earlobe and loved on to the pulsing cord in her neck, raising shivers through her flesh. She was on tiptoe, straining to achieve the physical absorption that seemed so necessary to ease the inner aching. When his hand spread along her ribs just below the uplift of a breast, her lungs stopped working.

With shock, Annette realized that she had no control over what was happening to her. Her actions and reactions were being dictated by emotion and sensation. Josh was the leader and she was the follower. Never in her life had she allowed someone else to lead the way unless she knew where they were going, but Josh was taking her to an uncharted mountain peak and he was setting the pace.

She drew back, resisting, unaccustomed to the dizzying heights. Her body quaked with small tremors. Josh felt them and let her feet touch flat ground while keeping her within the loose circle of his arms. She couldn't look at him, not when she was so vulnerable.

Gritty sand had worked its way inside the thin mesh of her stockings. To the side, Annette could hear the soft murmur of the Atlantic Ocean. Her hands were spread across the front of his chest, the thud of his heartbeat beneath her fingers and the ragged edge of his breathing. Nervously she moistened her lips, tasting him and being unsettled all over again.

"You don't practice what you preach, Josh!" She attempted a breezy accusation, but it came out breathless and disturbed.

"Why is that?" His hands lightly stroked the back of her ribs, caressing and distracting.

"You didn't think much of Craig's public display of affection, but here you are—with me—doing the very same thing." Of course, there was a difference. There wasn't a soul around, which also accounted for some of Annette's nervousness.

"We are exposed here," Josh agreed. "And I would much prefer to make love to you in private." Her heart rocketed in a combination of thrill and alarm. But again, he was setting the tempo—and he was making the decisions. "My suite faces the water. It's just a short walk from here."

Her breath was coming in uneven spurts as she pushed the rest of the way out of his arms with a husky laugh. "I said I wanted a *little* romance, Josh. I don't remember implying anything about a full seduction number by moonlight."

A silence lengthened as Annette moved to pick up her shoes. She shook out the sand inside them, feeling the watchfulness of his gaze. She had never felt so unsure of herself. The beach could have been made of quicksand. She wished Josh would say something, because she couldn't think of a thing. Her pulse accelerated like a race car when he approached her.

"I made a mistake about your age," Josh said, "but I wasn't wrong about your experience. You haven't taken that step into the bedroom yet. You've never slept with a man, have you?"

Annette felt uncomfortably warm. "I've heard that men snore." She tried to be flippant.

When he slipped a hand under her arm she stiffened apprehensively, but Josh's only intention was to guide her to the sidewalk. Once there he stopped but continued to hold on to her arm.

"Put your shoes on," he instructed.

The moon highlighted his features, allowing Annette to see his expression. She knew her passionate response and subsequent cold feet had given him cause for anger, but she couldn't find any sign of it. Under the circumstances Josh seemed remarkably tolerant of her hot-then-cold behavior.

The grip of his hand balanced her as she slipped on her shoes and hooked the strap behind her heel. She didn't feel quite so small with them on—literally or figuratively—since they seemed to return some of her poise.

"There are two ways people can learn how to swim," Josh said, and Annette gave him a puzzled look. The subject was totally out of place. "The quickest is to throw them into the deep end and hope their instinct for survival will get them safely ashore. But that's a severe shock to the system and it rarely turns out to be a pleasant experience."

He paused briefly and it began to sink in that he was speaking analogically, comparing swimming to making love. Annette felt her inner confusion and tension begin to ease with his words.

"On the other hand, a person can learn to

swim slowly," Josh continued. "It means starting out by practicing some of the basics and ad-
vancing by stages. Then it becomes an activity a
person can enjoy."

"Yes." Her smile was soft.

Because of his understanding, she fell a little
bit more in love with him. In his own way he was
telling her that he wanted her but he wasn't going
to rush her. It indicated a respect for her as a person. She wasn't merely a means to satisfy his lust.
If he respected her, Josh could love her, and that
was ultimately her aim.

"Let me pick up the champagne bottle and
glass, then I'll walk you to your room," he said
as he released her arm.

"Okay." Annette didn't object.

Her gaze followed his easy striding figure
across the sand to the spot where he had discard-
ed the bottle and the glass. She felt a little bit
starry-eyed and bemused. She had known Josh
was special the minute she'd seen him. And time
was proving her to be right.

When he returned, he hooked an arm around
her shoulders and curved her to his side. Their
legs brushed against each other as they started
walking slowly in the direction of her room. She
rather liked the feeling of his hard thigh rubbing
against hers, their steps matching. Simple things
brought quiet joy, but the sensation was no less
pleasing because of its simplicity.

Ahead of them a litter barrel was screened to
blend in with the landscape. They stopped so

Josh could deposit the champagne bottle and glass inside it. They left the beach area and entered the hotel grounds, following the sidewalk. Moonlight silvered the pavement to add its glow to the ground-lighted walk.

"Your sister doesn't resemble you, does she?" Josh remarked.

"No. We're a mixed-up combination of our parents," she smiled. "Marsha has my mother's eyes and fair complexion and dad's dark hair. I have his eyes and my mother's hair. And Robby's a whole different story. We are unique, to say the least."

"I would agree," he murmured, his downward glance vaguely mocking. "What happened to your mother?"

"She died when I was small. She had congenital heart trouble—nothing serious—but she caught the flu...and died," Annette explained. "For a long time it was just dad, Marsha and me...until we found Kathleen."

"You *found* Kathleen?" Josh questioned the choice of verbs.

"It's a long story," she assured him with a laughing smile. "To make it short, I guess you could say that Kathleen was hired to look after us—as a kind of nanny. After she and dad got to know each other, the rest, as they say, is history."

"You like her a great deal, don't you?" he observed.

"Yes." It was almost an understatement.

"She's mother, big sister and best friend all rolled into one. I couldn't have picked a better wife for my dad if I'd tried."

The statement slipped out before Annette realized she'd said it. She slid a brief glance at Josh to see if he read anything unusual in it. At this stage it was better he didn't know about the way she and Marsha had helped their father's courtship along. But Josh seemed to take the remark at face value.

When they reached the outside stairs to the second-floor balcony-hall where her room was located, he let his arm slide to her waist, giving each of them more freedom to climb the steps. They passed the corner suite occupied by her parents. The curtains were pulled and no light could be seen.

Before they reached the door to her room, Annette realized, "I forgot my key. I'll have to wake Marsha up to let me in."

"Either she's still awake or she left a light on for you," Josh said, drawing her attention to the glimmer of light behind the window draperies.

"She's probably reading," Annette guessed.

With silent mutual agreement, they stopped in front of her door and Annette turned, his hand sliding from the back of her waist to a rounded hipbone. There was a velvet quality to his look, warm and sensual. It had its effect on her senses, disturbing them in an inwardly thrilling way.

His hand increased its pressure on her hip to draw her closer, while the other tunneled under her hair to cup the back of her head. She raised her lips to his descending mouth and slid her arms inside his jacket to circle his middle. His male length was as hard and warm as his kiss—and as evocative. There was the instant leaping of desire, but Annette was prepared for it this time so its force didn't alarm her. Of her own accord she invited him to deepen the kiss. His hand shifted to her lower back and arched her firmly against him.

When he pulled his male lips from hers, there was a shaken edge to his rough breathing. His dark gaze blazed into her smoky eyes, black pupils dilated and ringed by a narrow gray iris.

"No more beginners' lessons for you," he stated huskily. "You're ready for the advanced courses."

"Think so?" she murmured, unconsciously provocative.

A bemused line turned in the corners of his mouth as Josh took his hand from her spine and knocked on the hotel-room door behind Annette. Getting the message, she loosened her encircling arms to stand free of him.

"Who is it?" Marsha's voice was partially muffled by the separating door.

"It's me—Annette," she answered reluctantly. "I forgot my key."

"Just a minute." The request was followed by the rattle of the safety chain and the turn of the dead bolt.

Before the door opened, Josh trailed a caressing hand across her cheek and let it pause to press his thumb to her lips and stroke them lightly. Then he was drawing it away.

"Good night, Annette," he murmured.

"Good night," she replied with equal softness.

He was walking away when the door swung in to admit Annette, but Marsha had a glimpse of his back before he disappeared. Her glance was sharp with curious interest when her older sister entered. She closed the door.

"You look positively mellow, Annette," she observed with some surprise. Her eyes widened as Annette made a waltzing circle across the floor and stopped, hugging her arms tightly around her.

"I'm in love," she laughed. "If I had any doubts, they vanished tonight!"

"I take it the lucky man is Josh," Marsha guessed. "What happened?"

"Nothing. Everything," Annette declared, apparently unaware of the extremes of her two answers. With a graceful turn she sank onto the bed and lay back on the pillows, fully dressed.

"Well, where did you go?" She wondered if her sister was capable of an answer that made sense. "What did you do?"

There wasn't an immediate reply, then Annette propped herself up on one elbow. Marsha didn't like the mischief dancing in her eyes.

"Josh invited me to his suite," Annette announced.

"Annette, you didn't go?" Even as she doubted, Marsha was prepared to believe almost anything. Sometimes she swore her sister delighted in shocking her with outrageous statements.

"No, I didn't go." She lay back on the pillows with that dreamy smile dominating her expression. "Not this time anyway."

Marsha forced herself to ignore the qualification, certain she was being baited. "Does he love you?"

The question had a sobering effect on Annette. "I'm not sure." She sighed heavily and stared at the ceiling. "It's so difficult to be objective. Sometimes I can't even think straight when he's near me," she admitted. "But if he doesn't love me now, he will—soon."

Marsha wasn't as positive about it, but she decided it was better if she kept her doubts to herself. Annette had a way of making things work out the way she wanted them to, even when Marsha thought it was impossible. For her sister's sake, she hoped it would be the case this time, too.

When Annette began telling her about Josh, Marsha moved to her bed and sat cross-legged at the bottom of it. She listened while Annette confided her excitement and fears and happiness. She wasn't sure how many yawns she smothered before Annette's exuberance abated. It was well into the wee hours of the morning before either of them crawled under the covers to sleep.

It seemed that Annette had barely laid her head on the pillow when the telephone began ringing shrilly. She tried burying her head under the pillow, but it couldn't shut out the incessant ring. Marsha groaned in the next bed.

Dragging an arm from beneath the covers, Annette groped for the phone on the bed table. Her fingers plucked the receiver off the hook in mid-ring and carried it under the pillow to her ear.

"Hello," she mumbled grumpily.

"Up and at 'em, sleepyhead," Josh's disembodied voice chided her.

Her eyes opened as she fought off the drugging tiredness. "Josh?"

"How many other men call you in the morning?" he mocked.

She sat up, knocking the pillow to the floor. "This is the first time you've called," Annette reminded him.

"So it is," he admitted. "Are you jogging with me this morning?"

"I . . . what time is it?" Between sleep and confusion, nothing was clear.

"Six-thirty."

Part of her wanted to collapse onto the mattress, but not the half in control. "I have to get dressed yet."

"Pity," he replied. "I'll give you fifteen minutes, then I'm leaving without you."

"I'll be ready." She was already throwing back the covers and swinging out of the bed. "Bye."

"Aren't you going to ask where to meet me?" Josh chided.

"Where shall I meet you?" she asked, obliging him.

"I'll wait for you at the beach."

"In fifteen minutes," she repeated.

"Now you can hang up," he mocked.

Smiling at the receiver, she did. As she started for the bathroom, Marsha groggily raised her head, giving her a blurry-eyed look.

"Where are you going? Who was that?" she muttered thickly.

"It was Josh. He wants me to go jogging with him," Annette explained hurriedly, and took off toward the bathroom.

"What time is it?" Marsha frowned.

Annette paused at the door long enough to answer, "Six-thirty."

With a groan, Marsha flopped her head onto the pillow. "You must be crazy," she mumbled, but water was running in the sink so Annette didn't hear when Marsha added, "or in love."

She was asleep when Annette left the room twelve minutes later to meet Josh.

THE NEXT FEW DAYS they seemed intent on making up for lost time. They jogged together in the mornings before Josh went to his office, then met again in the evenings. Annette stubbornly ignored her father's disapproving looks and thinly veiled remarks of displeasure at her choice of escorts. Sometimes they went out and sometimes they stayed around the hotel—at the beach or on his boat.

This night, Josh had taken her into Wilmington on the mainland. As they strolled along, Josh held her hand loosely within the clasp of his. It was a somnolent evening, the lengthening shadows of a retiring sun spreading over the city.

"Getting hungry?" he asked.

Her answer was a nod, followed by, "You mentioned something about eating around here."

"The restaurant's just ahead of us." Josh motioned toward a building they were approaching. "Do you like Mexican food?"

"I like tacos," Annette replied with a teasing sparkle in her glance.

"That's as bad as saying you like chop suey when someone asks if you enjoy Chinese food," he chided, but his look was warm with shared amusement.

"Do you mean there is more to Mexican food than tacos, enchiladas and refried beans?" She pretended to be surprised by the idea.

"Shall we go in and find out?" he challenged.

"Let's," Annette agreed. "I'm starving."

Mariachi music was playing in the background as a hostess led them to a table. The air was filled with a spicy blend of food smells that whetted Annette's already aroused appetite. Sitting down in one of the brightly colored chairs, she opened the menu and skimmed the list. She paused and glanced up at Josh.

"I think you'd better make some suggestions," she murmured.

"Why don't you trust me to order for you?" he suggested instead.

Annette hesitated, then agreed with a qualification. "All right, but tell me what it is."

The glint in his dark eyes mocked her, but he made no direct comment. He began his choice with guacamole salad, then a platter of assorted entrées so Annette could sample a variety. "Including the requisite taco," he informed her.

"At least I won't starve." She smiled her acceptance of his decision.

The order Josh gave the waiter included a carafe of sangría. The glasses that accompanied the chilled Spanish wine contained a speared slice of orange fruit and a stemmed maraschino cherry, which added to the fruity zest of the wine.

The emptiness of her stomach caused Annette to eye the fruit garnish hungrily. Finally, she gave up any attempt to resist it and slid the wine-soaked orange slice off its decorative spear to nibble on its pulp.

As her teeth sank into its orange flesh, her glance strayed to Josh. The raw hunger in his look centered on her juice-moistened lips as if he longed to devour them. The sensation was decidedly unnerving. It shivered through her, awakening her slumbering needs. She set the orange rind aside, inwardly aroused and unsettled by his looks.

"I wish you wouldn't look at me that way," she murmured.

"What way?" Thick masculine lashes were

partially lowered to screen the intensity of his gaze, but they didn't lessen his interest.

"As if you were eating me with your eyes," Annette replied, and twirled the cherry by its stem, drowning it in the wine.

"I'd like to take a bite out of you," Josh admitted with too much ease.

"Little nibbles are better," she replied, fully aware they were engaged in thinly disguised sexual banter. She flirted with him to conceal the fact she was affected by it.

"What are you going to do with that cherry?" His low question tied a knot in her stomach as her fingers stopped spinning the cherry in the wine.

"Do you want it?" Her tone wasn't as sophisticated as she wanted it to sound.

"What do you think?" He held her gaze and she felt the slow uncoiling of her tension under his steady look.

"You can have it." Holding the cherry by its stem, she handed it to him.

Instead of taking it, his fingers circled her wrist and guided her hand to his mouth so that she ended up feeding him the cherry. A thousand sensations ran through her system until she felt her toes curling in reaction, but nervousness wasn't one of her feelings.

The waiter approached the table to serve their meal and Josh released his hold on her wrist. Their conversation shifted to less suggestive topics, but the previous one wasn't forgotten. It lingered on the edge of her consciousness throughout dinner and afterward.

Arriving at the hotel, Josh parked the car in his reserved space and switched off the engine. When he stepped out of the car, Annette waited in the passenger seat until he had walked around and opened her door. She accepted his hand to help her out. Josh held on to it, keeping her at his side while he shut the door.

When he made no move to leave the shadowed lot for the lighted walkways, her heart started skipping beats all over the place. He faced her, his hand settling on her hip while he curved the hand he was holding behind his back and released it. He bent his head and nuzzled her mouth, arousing a trembling need for his kiss.

"Kissing in cars isn't very satisfactory." His low voice vibrated against her skin. "You can never get close enough."

Annette couldn't have agreed with him more as the weight of his body pressed her back against the side of the car. She was sandwiched between two unyielding shapes, the solid metal of the car and the living steel of his muscled form.

His mouth stopped teasing hers and parted her lips in driving possession. She could taste the heady blend of spicy food and fruity wine on his tongue, but Josh was feeding a different kind of hunger. And she echoed his need, incited by the hard male outline of his body imprinted on her soft flesh.

There was a roughness to the kisses he brushed over her neck and throat. His roaming hands were impatient with the restrictions placed upon them by her interfering clothes. Annette felt a similar frustration.

"This isn't enough for you, either, is it?" Josh demanded thickly.

"No." She was shaken by her extreme wants and willing to admit them.

A faint shudder went through him as he lifted his head and framed her face in his hands. His breathing was raggedly disturbed and desire smoldered in his eyes. Annette gazed at him with raw wonder.

"Let's go to my suite." The suggestion fell somewhere between a request and a command, insisting while giving her a choice.

"Yes." She was vaguely stunned that she could sound so calm when she had just made a momentous decision.

She hadn't been aware of his inner tension until she noticed the line of his jaw relax and felt the pressure of his hands lighten. Josh let her go long enough to curve an arm around her waist and direct her toward the hotel buildings. The contact provided support for her weak legs. Her mind was so filled with Josh, Annette wasn't conscious of thinking about anything else.

Another couple were strolling arm in arm along the sidewalk they approached. At first Annette looked at them without really seeing the man and woman, until recognition forced itself into an awareness. A finger of discomfort ran down her spine as she met her father's look.

"You're back earlier than we expected, Annette." His smile of greeting didn't reach his eyes. "I take it the two of you decided to have an early night."

"Not exactly. It's such a lovely evening we thought we'd walk around a bit." She certainly couldn't tell her father that she had been on her way to Josh's suite.

"Kathleen and I had the same thought," her father stated. "We can all go together."

With a sinking feeling, Annette looked at Josh with a questioning side-glance. The slight upward curve of his mouth held rueful humor and resignation.

"It sounds like a good idea," he told her father.

The four of them wandered through the hotel grounds together. Annette couldn't ever remember a time when her father had appointed himself as her chaperon on any dates. It seemed a little uncanny that he did it that night.

CHAPTER SEVEN

THE SAND WAS WARM beneath her as Annette leaned back on her hands and watched her small brother send the red Frisbee sailing through the air. Robby laughed in delight when Josh went chasing across the beach after it—all tanned sinewy legs and flatly muscled chest. The red disk landed in the sand. Josh scooped it up with one hand, spinning around in one movement and sailing it back in Robby's direction.

Her little brother tried to catch it and failed. When he tried to duplicate Josh's coordinated maneuver, he lost his balance and plopped on his bottom in the sand. Josh trotted over, panting slightly, and dropped down on one knee.

"Are you okay?" He lifted Robby to his feet and helped him brush off the sand.

"Yeah," Robby mumbled, a little embarrassed by the fall, since he had been trying to show off.

Josh rumpled the boy's dark hair. "Let's both take a rest."

"I'm not tired," Robby protested.

"But I am," Josh grinned. "You can play in the sand awhile and I'll do the resting."

"Okay," he agreed reluctantly to the suggestion.

While Robby went to get his sand bucket and shovel, Josh straightened and walked over to where Annette was sitting. Breathing out a tired sigh and smiling at the same time, he sank onto the beach beside her and clasped his arms around his knees. His gaze went back to Robby, busy packing sand into his bucket.

"I don't know where he gets the energy." Josh shook his head in weary amazement and slid an amused glance at Annette. "Does he ever run down?"

"About eight-thirty every night," she smiled. "I'm glad you didn't object to Robby's spending the afternoon with us."

Her father had taken Kathleen and Marsha shopping. Annette knew, from past experience, that Robby wasn't any fun to have along on shopping expeditions.

"Did you think I would?" he asked.

"No. But you could have."

She didn't mention her suspicion that this afternoon of baby-sitting her brother might have been concocted by her father. After last night's episode, she had the feeling he didn't want her to be alone with Josh. It was entirely possible that she was just imagining that, though.

Annette turned to lie on her stomach. She uncapped the bottle of suntan oil next to her beach towel and handed it to Josh. "Would you rub some on my back?"

"With pleasure."

Crossing her hands in front of her, she rested her cheek on them. An involuntary shiver danced over her skin when Josh dribbled the cool oil along her spine. His hands began spreading it around, gliding silkily over her back, almost caressing.

She closed her eyes as his strong fingers kneaded her shoulders, feeling her muscles relax under his gentle massage. "You can keep that up for at least another hour," she murmured.

"I can, huh?" His voice half challenged her. "I might get carried away with what I'm doing."

His mock warning was given credence when his hands shifted their attention to the sides of her rib cage. His fingertips made discreetly tantalizing forays under the edge of her white swimsuit to investigate the swelling curve of her breasts.

"You remind me of a slice of golden brown toast," Josh remarked. "All crisp and firm on the outside and soft and doughy in all the right places."

The rubbing motion ended as he drew away. Annette murmured a protest, but he playfully slapped her behind. "No more," he declared as she rolled onto her side in startled surprise, covering the stinging portion of her bottom with her hand.

"That hurt," she complained, even though the stinging sensation had already subsided.

"Shall I kiss it and make it better?" Josh teased, and caught Annette without a comeback.

Robby picked that opportune moment to join them. "Are you rested?" he inquired of Josh.

"Why don't you give me a few more minutes?" Josh asked.

"Okay," Robby sighed, and trotted off.

Annette watched him go, then glanced sideways at Josh. "Robby likes you."

Josh glanced after Robby, too, then back. One knee was bent, an arm resting on top of it. His other leg was stretched out on the sand, an arm braced behind him in support.

"Robby likes anybody who will play Frisbee with him," Josh replied.

"No." Annette shook her head. "He likes you. Robby is like me. He has an instinct for people. I've never known him to be wrong about anyone." She eyed Josh, admiring not just the outer man but the inner one, as well. "You'd be a good father."

"Is that right?" He turned to her, the arm leaving his knee to curve behind the middle of her back and pull her to him. He stopped when her swimsuit-covered breasts brushed against his chest. "Would you be interested in having my baby?" He asked the question against her lips and let them answer him by surrendering to the possession of his.

Love seemed to create an explosion of light inside her, spraying its brightness through every corner of her body. She wasn't conscious of Josh lowering her shoulders to the sand while he leaned over her to keep the intimate linkage of the kiss. She was dazed and aching when he dragged his mouth from hers. Dimly she heard the laughter and shouts of other bathers on the beach.

"I swear you are a witch," Josh accused her on a disturbed note.

"If I am, you must be a warlock," she murmured, because she knew how strong the spell had been, blocking out their surroundings— everything.

"We'll have dinner in my suite tonight," he stated.

For once, Annette didn't object to her lack of option. She simply nodded a silent acknowledgment of his plans. His gaze darkened at the movement, then he was letting her go to sit up.

"I think I'd better see what Robby is doing," Josh suggested dryly, indicating his awareness that the situation between them had grown too intense.

THERE WERE WITNESSES to the kiss other than the uninterested bathers on the beach. Poised on the steps overlooking the stretch of sand, Jordan Long stood watching. The line of his jaw and mouth was hard as iron. His gray eyes had darkened to a charcoal blackness. Kathleen and Marsha were on either side of him. Marsha was eyeing him with apprehension while Kathleen viewed him with resigned tolerance.

He pivoted away from the scene. "Come on," he instructed them to accompany him. "We're going to our rooms."

"I thought we were going to let Annette know

that we were back," Kathleen said, reminding him of their purpose in coming to the beach area.

"Not right now we're not. I'm liable to kill him with my bare hands." Jordan was rigid with parental outrage. "Did you see the way he kissed her?" he demanded. "Right out there in public!"

"Jordan," Kathleen attempted to reason with him patiently as they started toward their rooms, while Marsha trailed behind, out of range of her father's temper. "You have kissed me on a public beach before."

"Yes, I did! And you know damn well what I suggested afterward, too!" he reminded her with angry force.

"You are a hypocrite, Jordan." Kathleen couldn't help smiling at his indignation, although she tried not to let it show. "You want your daughters to do as you *say*, not as you *do*."

He stopped to confront her, his temper not improved by the glimmer of a smile in her expression. "I suppose you think I'm wrong," he challenged, "because I don't want my daughter seduced by some playboy."

"It isn't a question of whether you are right or wrong for being upset," she reasoned. "Annette is twenty years old now. There are some decisions you can't make for her anymore. It's time you started trusting her to make the right ones for herself."

"Trust Annette?" Jordan scoffed. "That girl gets herself into more trouble on purpose than most girls do accidentally. I wouldn't be surprised if she doesn't have some hare-brained scheme in mind right now. That worries me almost more than Joshua Lord does!''

"You're just guessing that she might." But Kathleen didn't deny the possibility.

Jordan swung his head around to pin Marsha with a look. She had been trying to be unobtrusive, but he hadn't forgotten she was there.

"What do you know about what's going on?" he demanded, aware that his younger daughter found it impossible to conceal anything for long, especially without Annette around to bolster her.

"Nothing like what you're thinking," she answered nervously.

His eyes narrowed. "And what am I thinking?"

"I don't know." She refused to speculate, but she did add an explanation of her remark. "I just meant that Annette and Josh haven't done anything." When her father continued to regard her narrowly, Marsha forced herself to be more explicit. "He hasn't made love to her or anything like that."

"I should hope not!" The words fairly exploded from him. Then he tempered his voice to a less furious level. "Just exactly what has Annette told you about Joshua Lord?"

Marsha shifted uncomfortably and tried to avoid an answer before she settled for one she thought might mollify him. "She says she loves him."

"God, no." He muttered the words and lifted his gaze heavenward.

"Jordan, don't you think 'you're overreacting?" Kathleen was beginning to get a little irritated with him. "Annette was bound to fall in love sometime. And I don't think she made a bad choice when she picked Joshua Lord to be that man."

"So far he hasn't proved it to me," he retorted.

"He doesn't have to prove it to you!" Some of her auburn temper was letting itself be heard.

"That's where you're wrong!" Jordan snapped. "I intend to put a stop to this little affair before it goes any further!"

In the next second he was striding away, leaving Kathleen and Marsha standing on the sidewalk. Marsha looked worried when she met her stepmother's glance. Kathleen let out her anger in a long sigh.

"He's really upset, isn't he?" Marsha grimaced. "He shouldn't have taken it out on you."

"Yes, he should," Kathleen smiled briefly. "Being a sounding board is also part of loving, although it isn't much fun. We are bound to disagree on occasions. This happens to be one of them, but it doesn't mean we love each other less because of it."

Reassured by Kathleen that no damage had been done, Marsha allowed a faint smile to appear. "I know you're right. I guess it's just that you and dad are always so happy together that it's a surprise to hear you argue."

"Shall we go to our room?" Kathleen suggested.

"Yes," Marsha agreed, and fell in step with her. "What do you suppose dad's going to do?"

"I have no idea," Kathleen admitted. "After he's calmed down, I'll talk to him again. I'm sure he'll listen to reason."

Marsha wasn't. Her father and Annette were a lot alike in that respect.

IN THE LATE AFTERNOON, Annette breezed into the hotel room. She had on a hooded caftan designed for beachwear. It added to her long leggy look.

"Hi." She smiled the airy greeting at Marsha. "Kathleen said you got back over an hour ago. Why didn't you let me know?" She didn't wait for an answer, rushing another question after the first. "What all did you buy?"

"Just a pair of slacks. They're hanging up in the closet," she said, and watched Annette with a guarded look. "When did you talk to Kathleen?"

"Just a couple of minutes ago." Annette walked to the closet to see Marsha's purchase. "I took Robby to his room to give him a bath and get him cleaned up before you guys got back. When I walked in with him, there were dad and Kathleen." She took out the hanger with the new slacks on it. "Hey, these are nice. Blue, of course. Your wardrobe is getting in a rut, Marsha."

Marsha picked at a loose thread in the bedspread. "Did dad say anything?"

"No." Annette glanced in her direction, suddenly noticing her sister's guarded attitude. "Why?"

"I just wondered." Marsha shrugged with too much indifference.

Annette knew there was something more to it than that. "What did you expect him to say to me?"

"Nothing," Marsha insisted.

"There must have been something or you wouldn't have asked," Annette persisted. "Now, what is it?"

"It's just that. . . we did go to the beach to let you know we were back early," she explained unwillingly.

Annette frowned. "But I didn't see you."

"No, but we saw you." Marsha paused and sighed. "Or rather, we saw Josh kiss you." Annette lifted her head a fraction of an inch, like an animal scenting trouble. "Dad was furious. That's why I thought he might have said something to you."

"He didn't." And she wondered why not.

"I guess Kathleen talked to him. She said she was going to. . . after he cooled down." Marsha offered that as an explanation.

"Maybe," she conceded, and removed the caftan by pulling it over her head. "I just don't understand why dad doesn't like Josh. He barely knows him."

"I think dad believes *you* barely know him," her sister pointed out.

"Well, he's wrong." She hung the caftan up in the closet and began sorting through her clothes. "You should have seen Josh today with

Robby. What do you think I should wear tonight?''

"Are you going out?" The minute she asked it, the question seemed totally ridiculous.

"Yes, I'm having dinner with Josh." Annette was careful not to mention where. "He's seen me in just about everything."

"Why don't you wear my blue silk dress?" Marsha suggested.

Annette turned, her face lighting up, but she didn't accept immediately. "Are you sure you don't mind? It's your favorite."

"No, go ahead," she insisted. "You'll look terrific in it."

"Thanks."

Reaching in the closet, she took out the azure-colored dress and carried it to the dresser mirror. She held the waistline against her bathing suit to see how it would look on her. Marsha was right. It was terrific—the fabric, the color, the style.

"Oh, Marsha, it's gorgeous," Annette breathed. "Thanks for letting me wear it. I promise I'll do the same for you anytime." Her expression became affectionate and thoughtful. "We may not be much alike for sisters, but you always come through when I need you."

"What are sisters for?" Marsha grinned.

CHAPTER EIGHT

ANNETTE WAITED until her family had gone to dinner before she left the room to walk to Josh's suite. Her stride was light and free. She could have been walking on air for all the notice she paid to the ground. It was a perfect July night—a soft breeze blowing in from the sea, night birds singing in the trees and a gorgeous sunset bleeding the sky with reds and oranges. She laughed aloud when she discovered she was humming to herself.

Arriving at the door to his suite, she knocked twice and waited, but not for long. She heard the approach of his footsteps and the turn of the lock before it was pulled open. Her bright gray eyes swept over him.

His white silklike shirt was unbuttoned at the throat, contrasting sharply with the bronze tan and hairy-rough texture of his skin. The cuffs of the sleeves were rolled back to reveal his forearms. Dark slacks were loosely molded to his slim hips.

The lazy half smile on his mouth disarmed her. "Right on time," Josh observed, and reached out to take her hand, inviting her in.

His suite was a self-contained apartment, complete with a living room, a dining area overlooking the bay, a kitchen and—naturally—a bedroom. Annette could see this last through an opened doorway.

The thick gold draperies were pulled to let the vibrant colors of the sunset spill into the suite. The white linen on the table reflected the scarlet hues of the setting sun. The table was set for two, polished silver shining and crystal goblets glittering. In the middle, a matched set of silver holders supported a pair of slim blue candles.

"I thought we'd eat later—after the sun goes down," Josh said, following the direction of her gaze.

"I agree. It would be a shame not to use the candles." And sunlight didn't seem nearly as romantic as candlelight, but Annette didn't feel she needed to say that.

"In the meantime we can have some champagne." Josh led her by the hand into the living room. "This time it will be properly chilled," he added, obliquely referring to the tepid wine they'd drunk on the beach.

Releasing her hand, he lifted the bottle out of the bucket of ice on the coffee table. A pair of wineglasses sat on a tray. Annette picked them up while Josh attempted to work the cork out of the bottle. It defied him at first, then the pressure inside shot the cork into the air, ricocheting it off the ceiling. Frothy wine bubbled from the neck. Annette quickly held out a glass to catch the overflow.

"Aren't you lucky I was prepared?" she laughed. By some miracle not a drop was spilled.

"I knew you would be," Josh replied, and set the bottle deep in the nest of ice. Facing her, he touched the rim of his wineglass to hers, the fine crystal making a tinkling chime at the light contact. "To the rest of the evening," he toasted softly.

"To the rest of the evening," Annette murmured, and carried the glass to her lips, sipping the sparkling wine and holding his gaze over the clear rim. The bubbles tickled her throat. She had to cover her mouth to contain a choking cough, trying to laugh at her predicament. "I knew those bubbles would get me someday," she said hoarsely, when she was able to talk again. "But I always thought I would embarrass myself by sneezing."

"I can't imagine anything embarrassing you," Josh replied.

"It takes a lot," she admitted in a more natural voice.

"Come on." He slipped an arm around her waist. "Let's sit on the couch."

Skirting the coffee table in front of it, Josh guided her to the sofa cushions. When they were both seated, his arm was around her shoulders, curving her to his side. His body heat warmed her skin, sensitizing her nerve ends to the solid feel of his flesh.

It seemed impossible to be more aware of him, but she was. Yet there wasn't any nervousness, even though this was the first time she'd ever been alone with a man in his apartment. She had attended parties before at a male friend's place, but there had always been a horde of other friends there, as well.

"What are you thinking about?" Josh asked, his gaze playing over her features.

"How comfortable I am," she admitted, and took another sip of champagne. This time she didn't choke on the bubbles.

"You managed that without a cough or a sneeze," he observed. "Your glass is nearly empty. Shall I refill it for you?"

"No," Annette refused. "I hadn't better have any more on an empty stomach. It goes to my head too quickly, and you'd wind up with a slightly tipsy blonde at dinner."

"Very sensible," Josh murmured, and drank from his glass.

Her glance studied the tanned column of his throat as he swallowed the wine. Her fingers curled with the desire to touch him, but she kept them around the stemmed crystal glass.

"If you'd like to pour yourself some more, don't let me stop you," she offered.

"Why? Do you want me to get 'slightly tipsy'?" He mocked her with her own phrase.

"That's an interesting thought," she murmured provocatively.

A low chuckle came from his throat. "And I always thought the man was supposed to get the girl drunk."

"Turnabout is fair play," Annette countered

with a half shrug, the weight of his arm lessening the movement.

"Is it?" He set his glass down on the end table, then took hers and placed it beside his. "In that case, you can kiss me."

She started to laugh, then realized Josh was serious. On second thought, she rather liked the idea of being the one to initiate an embrace. The hand that had been so anxious to touch him curved itself to the ropy muscles along his neck, applying pressure to bend his head to hers.

Her lips mobilely found the warmth of his and it ceased to matter who was the aggressor. Josh was turning to her, his hand reaching for her. It seemed he was burying his mouth in hers, filling all the intimate recesses. His thin shirt was like a second skin; her caressing hands had all the sensation of touch of his muscled shoulders and back. Latent power rippled beneath her fingers.

She was drunk on the taste of him and it affected all the rest of her senses. Wild vibrations swept her as Josh nuzzled her neck and rediscovered the sensitive pulse point at the base of her throat. The wayward roaming of his hands was creating a havoc of its own, exciting and arousing her to a fever pitch.

His hand slid along her thigh, trying to mold her to him. "This is as bad as a car," Josh sighed in frustration, and lifted her onto his lap.

The kissing and caressing continued with greater freedom. Her hands made a tactile exploration of his hewed features, memorizing the cut of his jaw and the curve of his cheekbone and discovering the softness of his thick lashes. Lengthening shadows outside darkened the room as twilight purpled into night. Josh stirred, a hand smoothing the hair near her face.

"Are you hungry?" It was a very reluctantly issued question.

"No." And she wondered if he had wanted her to say yes.

"Good." Josh gave her the answer, a fire slumbering in his dark eyes. "I wasn't looking forward to making love on a full stomach."

The breath disappeared from her lungs. His arms tightened to keep her cradled against him as he rolled to his feet. Her hands automatically linked themselves around his neck. Familiarity with his surroundings allowed Josh to carry her to the bedroom without the benefit of a light.

Inside the room, he let her stand. His hands settled onto the soft points of her shoulders, kneading them lightly. Her heart was thudding against her ribs as Josh bent his head and kissed her with warm slow desire. Annette swayed toward him, but his hands kept her away. Lifting his head, he looked at her deeply.

With a slight pressure, he turned her in a half circle. His hands moved and Annette closed her eyes as they glided down her back, unzipping her dress. They came back to slide it off her shoulders, letting it fall to the floor. The semidarkness of the room added to the sensation of intimacy as Josh undressed her.

He carried her to the bed and stripped back the covers to lay her on the silkiness of the sheets. Kissing her, he sat on the edge of the bed, leaning to her. His hands made restless trails over her softly full curves, tingling her flesh wherever they touched.

When he straightened to sit erect, Annette reached out a hand, letting it trail over his hair-roughened chest. Josh finished unbuttoning the shirt and removed it, tossing it aside. His skin felt hot to the touch, on fire, as she was. The touch of her hand compelled him back to her.

His mouth rocked over hers, then wandered to the pulsing vein in her neck. Her hands moved restlessly over his shoulders, fingers running in and out of his thick hair. A quivering rush of emotion swelled within her when his hand cupped the roundness of a breast. As his mouth made a foray over its nubile peak, Annette sunk her teeth into her lower lip to silence the wanton murmurs of delight. His hard male lips came back to her throat as if to investigate the faint sounds.

"You are so incredibly beautiful, Annette," he murmured huskily.

His words broke the lock she'd placed on her own voice. "I love you, Josh," she whispered with overwhelming certainty.

He was motionless for an instant, his mouth against her skin but not caressing. Slowly he levered himself a foot away from her. Even in the darkness she was conscious of his gaze searching her face. At first she thought he didn't believe.

her. Her lips parted to reaffirm the statement.

But Josh spoke first, a rather weary, "I should have known." He sat the rest of the way up.

Annette was bewildered. "What do you mean?" she murmured. He hadn't turned away from her or stopped looking at her.

"Why did you choose this particular minute to say that?" he asked.

"Because it's what I feel." She frowned her confusion. "I thought I should tell you."

"But why now?" Josh persisted.

"What difference does it make?" She didn't understand what possible significance that had. A coolness began to drift over her naked flesh without the arousing warmth of his hands to shut it out. "You aren't making any sense." She didn't like being on the defensive. And why did she have to defend her love for him? "Why are you cross-examining me? What's your reason for subjecting me to the third degree all of a sudden?" she challenged him.

"And I'm questioning your motive for declaring your love for me at that precise moment," Josh replied grimly, and reached over to switch on the lamp by the bed.

It bathed Annette in its light, suddenly making her self-conscious of her nudity when she hadn't been before. Instinct had her reaching for the covers and pulling them over her to hide her nakedness from his eyes.

"There wasn't any motive," she protested. "I just wanted to tell you."

Looking at him in the light, she could see the effects of their lovemaking. His mahogany-dark hair was rumpled from her raking fingers. Passion continued to lurk in the corners of his velvet brown eyes. There was a sensual fullness to his masculine lips, a direct result of their many kisses. Yet he wasn't holding her or touching her or making any attempt to eliminate the small distance between them in the bed.

"I suppose you didn't have it in mind to declare your love just before we had sex for the first time in order to implant a subconscious guilt in me because I was taking your virginity." The quietness of his voice seemed to carry an accusing ring. "Afterward were you hoping to make use of that guilt by applying a little emotional blackmail to persuade me to marry you?"

"No." Annette denied the allegation. "I didn't have anything like that planned."

"Then you aren't expecting me to marry you?" Josh asked for a clarification.

That was one she couldn't give. It caused her to falter, betraying herself. She looked at him, searching his features for some sign of emotion for her.

"Don't you want to marry me?" she murmured with a sinking heart.

"No." His reply was brutally simple.

"But—" A hard lump welled in her throat. Annette had to pause to swallow it. "I thought. . . ." She tried again. "This afternoon you asked if I would be interested in having your baby."

A wry kind of amusement flickered across his features. "Annette, that was another way of asking to make love to you," he explained with droll patience. "That is how babies are made, but I have absolutely no intention of getting you pregnant."

To her shame, Annette realized she had read into his question something he hadn't meant at all. She, who had prided herself on being so clever, had just made an incredibly stupid error. She felt sick. She stared at the sheet, her eyes burning with hot tears that wouldn't fall.

"I didn't understand what you meant," she admitted stiffly.

"You know I've made love to other women in the past," Josh stated his own experience. "Haven't you considered how many other women have lain in this bed with me?"

Part of her wanted to cover her ears to shut out the things he was saying. And another part wanted out of the bed he had shared with someone else. It made her feel unclean.

"No, I haven't." There was a hoarseness in her voice. "I thought I was different...special." The bitterness of self-conceit coated her tongue.

"Because you are a virgin?" Josh took a deep breath and released it in a heavy sigh. "Annette, men have had virgins before, and not married them."

"All...all you wanted was an affair." She nearly choked on the word, still unable to look at him, her stomach churning.

"Yes."

"Why didn't you tell me that?" Annette protested on a surge of anger.

"Because, until this afternoon, I thought you knew," he replied.

"Well, I didn't!" she flashed. "Where are my clothes? I want my clothes."

The mattress shifted beneath her as Josh stood up and walked to her pile of clothes in the middle of the floor. He took his time picking them up, then held them, his hand moving as if he were mentally weighing them. Returning to the bed, he offered them to her. Annette felt hot under his steady regard. One hand clutched the covers while she reached out with the other to snatch her clothes from his hand.

"Turn around so I can get dressed," she ordered harshly.

Josh shook his head in mocking amazement. "It's a little late for modesty, Annette. What more could I possibly see that I haven't already seen?"

"Just turn around," she said, because the circumstances were vastly different to her.

His mouth curved in a humorless line of resignation and he turned his back to her. Annette slipped from beneath the covers and began hurriedly to dress. She was unbearably conscious of Josh standing nearby, naked from the waist up. Even though he wasn't watching her she was uncomfortable. Yet something was nagging at her—something Josh had said that didn't make sense.

She was about to pull the dress over her head when she remembered. Stopping, she brought the dress down and stood there in her slip. Her gaze slid to his wide shoulders and tapered back.

"Why did you say that you thought I knew you were only interested in an affair *until this afternoon*?" She stressed the time frame.

"After I left you today, I had a visitor," he replied.

"Who?" Annette demanded. "Why should that have made a difference?"

Impatience rippled through his frame. "This is ridiculous," he muttered. "I'm not going to talk to the wall. Whether you like it or not, I'm turning around." Josh pivoted to face her, his gaze automatically raking her partially clad figure.

"Who came to see you?" Annette repeated the question, a gnawing suspicion already forming, but she wanted to be wrong.

"Your father," Josh answered.

She felt as if a thousand-ton weight had just landed on her. Her head moved to the side in a dull reaction. "He came to see you?" She didn't want to ask why.

"He wanted to find out my intentions toward you," he said, explaining the reason for her father's visit, one she had already guessed. "It came as a shock when he suggested you were thinking in terms of marriage, since the possibility never crossed my mind."

She wished Josh wouldn't keep repeating that.

"Why didn't you tell me about my father's visit when I arrived here tonight?"

A wryness stole across his expression. "Because I wanted you. So—" one shoulder lifted in an expressive shrug "—I half convinced myself that your father didn't know what he was talking about. I think fathers would sometimes prefer their girls to become nuns. I told myself that he made up this marriage thing because he couldn't accept the idea of your having an affair." Josh paused to study her. "It didn't occur to me that you didn't know the score."

"Until I said that I loved you," Annette remembered, unable to make up her mind whether she wished she could retract those words. She was hurting inside and the backlash from the pain was anger.

"That was the wrong timing," he said. "You wanted me to say I loved you then, didn't you?"

"Only if you meant it," she retorted, and yanked the dress over her head, pulling the skirt past her hips with a careless regard for the rich silk material.

"A lot of men would say it without meaning it, just to get you in their bed. I probably even did it when I was younger, but it ultimately creates too much hassle," Josh told her with steady calm. "The minute you said that, I knew your father was right. Marriage was part of your plans for us."

Her fingers tugged at the recalcitrant zipper behind her back, trying to force it to close. Frustration brought a latent violence to her actions. She wanted to get dressed and get out of there. She was trembling from the combination of pain and anger.

"Let me do that before you break the zipper," he volunteered roughly, and walked toward her.

At the touch of his hands, Annette jerked away from him. "I can do it." Her gray eyes blazed with the reflected anger of deep hurt. "I don't need your help."

The grip of his hands was firmly insistent as he overpowered her objections and turned her back to him. "Just shut up and let me do it, Annette. It will be a lot faster this way," he stated.

That was a very persuasive argument. She stood rigidly, fighting the sensation of his touch on her lower spine. Within seconds, the quiet sound of the closing zipper was traveling up her back.

"Do you want me to fasten the little hook at the top?" Josh asked.

"No." She stepped away from him. The dress was secure without the benefit of that finishing touch. She looked around for her shoes.

"Be honest, Annette," Josh challenged. "You were willing to go to bed with me because you thought I'd be so crazy about you, and so honored—" the inflection in his voice put a question mark at the end of that word "—to be the first that I would marry you. Isn't that how you planned for it to go?"

"Yes!" she hissed the bitter admission. She

hated feeling the fool—naive and disgustingly sophomoric.

"You must have read too many romantic stories," he decided.

"I must have," she agreed coldly, and scooped her shoes off the carpeted floor.

Agitation seemed to steal her natural grace. When she tried to put her shoes on, she had to hop in an ungainly fashion to keep her balance. It was one more humiliating blot on the evening.

"I'm sorry it turned out this way, Annette," Josh offered a grim apology.

"You should have told me you were scared of marriage," she lashed out at him, wanting him to feel small the way she did.

"I'm not afraid of marriage." A faintly indulgent smile touched the corners of his mouth, as if guessing what she was trying to do and regarding it as juvenile. "But when the day comes, it's going to be my choice. I'm not going to be maneuvered into it by some scheming little blonde."

"I got the message!" Annette snapped, not needing Josh to keep repeating it. "Besides, you can't maneuver anyone unless they are willing to be maneuvered."

"At least you know that much," he murmured the taunt.

"Look!" she flared. "You've made it clear you aren't interested in me! You don't have to keep rubbing it in!"

"If you think that, I haven't made it clear." His voice stayed level. "I am interested in you.

I'd like you to stay here tonight. I'd like to make love to you," he stated. "But what I'm not interested in is waking up tomorrow morning with a knock on the door and your father standing outside with a shotgun and a preacher, and you wailing that I've taken advantage of you. I can do without that scene."

"So can I!" she insisted, pride storming to the front.

"Good, then we can both be spared that." A little hardness formed along his jaw, his eyes darkening. "And the next time a man asks you to go to bed with him, make sure you do it because it's what you want, and don't think because he takes your virginity that he wants to marry you."

"I'll remember that." Annette was nearly spitting from the raw hurt raking her insides. "And you can bet your life that you won't be that man!"

A grim kind of anger tightened his mouth. "Am I supposed to feel deprived by that remark?" Josh demanded. "Are you trying to goad me into feeling possessive about you? You're still hoping to arouse some sort of declaration from me, aren't you?"

Was she? Annette didn't honestly know what she was trying to accomplish anymore. Except, maybe, she wanted him to feel some sense of loss, because she felt destroyed. It wasn't fair that she was the only one in the throes of pain.

"No!" She fiercely denied his claim. "I don't want anything from you! Not your kisses! Not your love! Nothing!'' But even as she said it, she knew they were lies. All lies. And she hurt all the more.

His head moved to the side in a mild form of quiet exasperation. "As I said before, I'm sorry it turned out this way. Maybe we'll meet again sometime.''

"Yes." Her throat muscles constricted from the seething churning agony inside. "Maybe we will—after I've had a couple of affairs so we can meet on common ground.''

"Annette—" his mouth thinned "—I'm letting you go—"

"You're not letting me go!" She choked with rage at the implication that he was *allowing* her to leave. "I'm walking out!''

It was the best exit line she'd had. Annette used it, whirling away to march from the bedroom. The blood was roaring in her ears. It was so loud that she couldn't hear if Josh was coming after her. She tried to pretend she didn't want him to. Another knife of pain was plunged into her heart when she reached the front door of his suite and realized Josh hadn't followed her.

Inside she felt ripped apart, shredded into pieces. The primitive rage of a wounded animal spread through her as she crossed the hotel grounds. She wanted to lash out, strike back, attack the person responsible for this.

Her irrational mind reminded her that her father had precipitated this whole incident with his visit to Josh. It was his fault it had all come to an abrupt end before she had a chance to make Josh love her. It could have worked.

The two men she cared the most about had hurt her. And Annette wanted to get back at them. The ever resurgent pain in her body insisted on it, blindly driving her into action without time to allow her to consider the lack of justification.

Reaching the door to her father's suite, Annette pounded on it with her fist. All the pent-up pain trembled violently through her. The hammering became an outlet of partial release. She kept it up even after she'd heard her father's muffled voice respond.

"Just a minute," he called in vague irritation.

Her fist hit the door one last time before it was swung open. Her burning eyes looked at her father's frowning expression as he paused in the midst of tying a knot in his robe's belt. Gray eyes, like hers, took in the whiteness of her complexion and the tremors that shook her.

"Annette!" His exclamation of concern quickly turned to a building anger. "What happened? What did he try to do?" His hands reached out to pull her inside the suite of rooms. "So help me God, I'll—"

With a violent shrug of her arms, Annette flung aside his hands. "How dare you!" she stormed. "Who gave you the right to talk to Josh about me?"

His head lifted at the attack, stiffening. "I'm your father. That gives me every right."

"No, it doesn't! You had no business interfering in my personal life!" Annette raged at him. "It has nothing to do with you! Don't you ever do it again!"

"You are my daughter," he began, as Kathleen hurried anxiously to his side.

"And don't think I'm not sorry about that! I wish I'd never been born! You're to blame for that, too!" She tried to ease her hurt by saying every cruel thing she could think of. Hot tears were finally spilling from her eyes and running down her cheeks.

"Keep your voices down, both of you," Kathleen ordered. "You're going to wake up Robby."

"I don't care!" Annette insisted, not attempting to lower the volume of her voice. "It's time he found out what kind of a father he has!"

"Young lady, you better watch your tongue," her father warned.

THE HOTEL WALL that separated the suite from Marsha's and Annette's room was not thick enough to silence the raised voices. Marsha was propped in a sitting position by the pillows on her bed, listening to them, the paperback novel in her hands forgotten.

She didn't understand why every time her sister and father argued that it had to turn into a shouting match. Her shoulders hunched at all that anger coming through the wall. Robby started crying to add to the furor.

Some loud remark from Annette was punctuated by the slamming of a door. A sudden silence followed. The argument was over and Marsha trembled with relief. Angry footsteps approached the door; a key rattled in the lock. Marsha started to get out of bed to open the door for her sister, but it was swinging in.

Annette swept in on a wave of temper and banged the door shut. She didn't say a word. She didn't even look at Marsha as she crossed the room and began undressing with jerky agitated movements.

This brooding silence always followed blistering arguments. Marsha had learned it was better to leave her sister alone if she didn't want to receive the broadside of her temper. Quietly she walked to the door and relocked it for the night.

Under the covers again, Marsha picked up her book and pretended to read it while she listened to Annette going through the motions of getting ready for bed. When Annette crawled into the twin to her bed, Marsha glanced hesitantly in her direction.

"Would you like me to turn off the light?" she asked.

"I don't care," Annette answered coldly.

Sighing her futile concern, Marsha set her book aside and switched off the lamp by the bed. For a long time she lay there trying to piece together the fragments of the argument she'd heard. It had been something about their father talking to Josh.

There were times when she envied Annette's bold confidence and thirst for adventure. But she was very glad she wasn't Annette right now. Rolling onto her side, Marsha closed her eyes.

CHAPTER NINE

ALL THE WHILE Marsha dressed the next morning, Annette lay in bed with her hands pillowed under her head, staring at the ceiling. There was no expression on her face, but Marsha wasn't deceived. There was raw pain in her sister's eyes and a glittering of anger. Those busy wheels in Annette's mind were turning, and Marsha was leery of all that implied.

She couldn't take the silence anymore. "Aren't you going jogging this morning?" she asked.

"No." The line of her jaw was hard and decisive.

Marsha hesitated, biting at her inner lip. "Do you want to talk about it?" She eyed her sister, feeling certain that Annette shouldn't keep it all bottled up inside like that.

"No, I don't want to talk about it." Not once did her gaze stray from the textured pattern of the ceiling.

There was a knock at the door and Marsha went to answer it. Kathleen was standing outside when she opened the door. She smiled and glanced past Marsha, spying Annette in the bed.

"We're on our way to breakfast," Kathleen

said. "If you're ready, we might as well walk together."

"I haven't brushed my hair yet," Marsha answered. "I'll be a few more minutes." She glanced over her shoulder toward Annette, who was still in the same position.

"Aren't you coming, Annette?" Kathleen asked.

"No." The answer was flat, allowing no opening for a discussion.

"Annette, I know how you feel—" Kathleen began, the warmth of understanding mixing with a firmness in her voice.

"No, you don't know how I feel." Annette cut across her words with a hard incisive stroke.

There was a trace of impatience in Kathleen's eyes as she glanced at Marsha. "She'll be all right," Marsha murmured the assurance. "She just needs a little time."

"Maybe we all do," Kathleen responded in an equally subdued tone.

"Go ahead to breakfast," Marsha urged. "I'll join you as soon as I'm ready."

Kathleen nodded a silent agreement and turned away. Quietly Marsha closed the door and turned to walk back toward the beds.

"You really should have some breakfast, Annette," she advised.

"Marsha, please," her sister flashed in exasperation. "I don't need any lectures from you about diet or exercise. Just go."

"I just thought you might feel better if you had

something to eat," Marsha retorted with a little
trace of anger at the undeserved snap.

"I'll eat later." Annette was less abrupt this
time, retreating into her thoughts and shutting
Marsha out.

There was the consolation that sooner or later
Annette would talk to her, but it was the only
consolation Marsha had as she entered the bathroom to brush her hair.

DARK SUNGLASSES SHIELDED HER EYES from the
glare of the afternoon sun as Annette lazed in a
lounge chair by the pool. Her indolent pose was a
farce. She continued to seethe inside, a churning
caldron of pain and anger and revenge.

Out of the corner of her eye she saw someone
approaching her chair. She turned to watch Craig
walking toward her. Dressed in his waiter's uniform, he had a stiff look of reserve in his expression, polite and nothing more. She wasn't really
surprised by his lack of friendliness, considering
the way she had ignored him lately because of
Josh. That was something she had to overcome.

He stopped beside her chair. "Jack said you
asked to see me." Jack was the other waiter who
had been on duty at the poolside.

Swinging her feet to the paved sun deck, Annette sat sideways in her chair and tipped her
glasses to perch atop her sun-streaked hair. As
she stood up she gave him her most alluring
smile.

"Yes, I did," she admitted, then looked

around at the other guests by the pool before returning her gaze to him. "Is there someplace private where we can talk?"

Interest flickered across his handsome face, then his eyes narrowed slightly. "I suppose there's something you want to find out about Josh Lord." He guessed at the reason she was paying attention to him.

"Josh is a bore," she declared with a coy little moue, wrinkling her nose. "So I certainly don't want to talk about him."

His expression began to unbend, that old charm gleaming in his eyes. Craig puffed up a little at the idea Annette might prefer him to Joshua Lord and all his money. Annette was almost disgusted at how easy it was if a girl pandered to a man's conceit.

"There's a place behind the game room. It's kind of secluded and out of the way. We could talk there," Craig suggested.

The game room was where all the pinball machines and electronic games were, adjacent to the pool area. It sounded ideal—quickly accessible and little chance of being observed. And she wanted to get this conversation over with.

"I'll gather up my things and discreetly follow you over there." The lilt in her voice seemed to promise him a special treat.

"Okay." Craig was smiling now. "I'll meet you there."

There was something almost leering in the way his gaze traveled over her white swimsuit. But nothing could penetrate the shell she'd erected to protect her pain-riddled senses and shattered soul.

As he ambled off in the direction of the game room, Annette bent to pick up her beach robe and bag. She took her time folding them to lie smoothly over her arm, then set off after him. When she walked around the corner of the game room, Craig was standing next to the building waiting for her.

"What happened between you and Josh Lord?" he asked curiously. "You two seemed to be a pretty hot item."

"There were a few things we didn't agree on, so I walked," Annette shrugged, and sauntered closer. "He didn't have anything worthwhile that you don't have." She stopped and ran her finger along the underside of his uniform's lapel, peering up at him. "Besides, I think you and I could' have more fun. That is—" she paused as though she might be too presumptuous "—if you'd still like to go out with me."

"Sure," he answered quickly, then tried to conceal his eagerness. "It might be fun."

"Are you busy tonight?" Annette continued to let her finger ride under his lapel, slowly going up and down.

"I was thinking about going over to a buddy's place. He's having a keg party. You're welcome to come along." Craig made it sound like he was doing her a favor by inviting her.

"Actually," she sighed, and her finger stopped

its movement, "I thought we could go somewhere a little more...private. Someplace where we could be alone, just the two of us. Do you know what I mean?"

"Like...uh...where?" His hand moved to the bare curve of her waist where the cut-out sides of her swimsuit exposed tanned skin.

"Maybe at your place—or a friend's?" Annette suggested.

"The guy I room with is...entertaining company tonight," Craig replied, eliminating that possibility. "And the one friend who might let me use his place is having the party."

"There must be someplace we can go," she reasoned.

"One of my buddies is a night clerk over on motel row." He studied her closely as he passed on the information. A motel sounded a little sordid, but Annette supposed it wouldn't matter.

"Wouldn't it be all booked up this time of year?" she asked, letting him know by her question that she was willing.

"It's policy to hold one room back for regular customers—businessmen who come here a lot," Craig explained. "He owes me a favor," he bragged. "What time do you want to meet, and where?"

"Is nine o'clock too late?" She allowed his hand to draw her against his length but arched her back a little to keep some space between them.

"That's fine," he agreed. "How about if I pick you up by the parking-lot exit?"

"I'll be there at nine o'clock on the dot," Annette promised, and kissed him lightly on the mouth, then slipped out of his hold, leaving him wanting more and expecting it. She waved to him and walked around the corner of the game room.

BENDING DOWN, Marsha gave Robby a hug and a good-night kiss. "See you in the morning," she promised. "Have a nice night and don't let the bedbugs bite," she teased, then straightened. "Good night, dad, Kathleen."

They echoed her parting phrases as she left them to walk to her own room. Unlocking the door, she walked in. A tray of dirty dishes sat on the round table by the window. Marsha guessed that her sister had ordered dinner from room service, since she had refused to have the evening meal with the family.

"Annette?" she called.

"I'm in the bathroom," her sister answered.

The door was standing open so Marsha walked over. Annette was leaning close to the lighted mirror and applying dark brown mascara to her lashes. Marsha stared at the haltered pink sundress and white sandals her sister was wearing.

"Are you going out?" Marsha asked in disbelief.

"Yes. I have a date." Annette stepped back to survey the finished product in the mirror.

"But...I thought you and Josh—" Marsha began in bewilderment.

"I'm not going out with Josh," her sister stat-

ed in the flat voice that had become her trade-
mark in the past twenty-four hours. "That's
over. We didn't have the same end in mind and
there wasn't any way to compromise."

"Then who—"

"Am I going out with?" Annette finished the
question for her. "Craig."

"Craig," Marsha repeated, because it didn't
sound possible. "The waiter?"

"Yes." Annette brushed past her into the main
section of the room. Dazed by the unexpected an-
nouncement, Marsha followed.

"But I thought you didn't like him." As a matter of fact, her sister had made it plain that she
didn't. But she'd never known Annette to do anything without a reason. There was bound to be
one this time. A thought occurred to her. "Are
you trying to make Josh jealous?"

"No." Annette laughed at the suggestion, but
there was little amusement in the sound. It was
too brittle and phony.

"Then why are you going out with Craig?"
Marsha frowned.

Annette made a project out of being certain the
room key was in her purse. "I never realized what
a problem it was being a virgin," she said airily.
"I've decided to eliminate it."

Marsha's mouth dropped open in shock. "You
aren't serious?" she protested on a squeak. "You
don't expect me to believe that you cold-bloodedly
intend to—"

"Take it from me," Annette interrupted, "the

cold-blooded way will cause a lot less heartache than the hot-blooded one. At least, you won't want—or expect—the man to marry you afterward."

Marsha didn't like that kind of logic, but she was beginning to understand what had happened between Annette and Josh. "But don't you want to—"

"Save myself for the man I marry?" Again Annette finished the sentence for her in a mocking tone. "The problem is the man I want doesn't want to marry me."

"But...surely Craig doesn't know what you have in mind?" Marsha was in a state of shock. She couldn't believe her sister was saying these things—or really intended to do them. .

"He's very dense if he doesn't," Annette retorted, suddenly sounding impatient. "What else would he think I wanted when I agreed to go to a motel with him?"

"A motel?" Marsha was shocked, appalled. This couldn't be her sister talking. It was someone else. "Annette, you aren't going there? It's so...so...."

"The place doesn't make any difference, Marsha." Impatience and irritation seemed to lace every word. "You've been reading too many romantic stories." She used the same accusation that Josh had directed at her. "Why don't you grow up for a change?"

Annette had criticized her before, but this time there was more sting to the barbs. "You talk about me growing up and you're the one who's going to some sleazy motel—''

"It isn't sleazy," Annette denied. "It's one of the places on motel row. Craig has a friend who's a night clerk." Her features became cloaked with cynicism. "He'll probably get the room for nothing."

"You can't go through with this," Marsha said flatly, suddenly very calm and determined.

"I can and I will," Annette stated, and started for the door.

Marsha rushed to block the way. "I mean it, Annette. You aren't thinking straight," she stated. "You're upset because of Josh and you want to hurt him, but you're going to end up hurting yourself more. If you'll think about it, you'll admit I'm right."

For a fleeting second there was a crack in her sister's defensive shell and Marsha had a glimpse of stark pain, but the slight break was immediately repaired. There was a stubborn set to Annette's jaw. She realized that she was determined to go through with this. Marsha could talk until she was blue in the face and not sway her from this self-destructive course she'd set.

"Would you mind getting out of my way?" Annette requested with stiff formality. "I don't want to keep Craig waiting."

There wasn't any way Marsha could stop her short of physical force, and even that was doubtful. Reluctantly she stepped to the side, letting Annette pass. She felt helpless as she watched her sister walk to the door and pause.

"Don't wait up for me," Annette declared with deliberate flippancy, and Marsha wanted to scream at her not to go. But she didn't.

"You're a fool," she said quietly instead.

The instant the door closed behind her, it unlocked the agitation that had been building inside Marsha. She ran a hand through her glistening brown hair, searching for some way she could stop her sister when reason had failed. She couldn't just let it happen.

Her mind recalled a remark Annette had made not long ago. "You're always there when I need you most," she'd said. Whether Annette knew it or not, she needed Marsha now. But what could she do? How could she help? She wished for Annette's cleverness at coming up with ideas. Time was slipping away.

It was out of the question to go to their father. After the angry quarrel they'd had, there was too much chance that involving him in this would lead to another with more severe consequences. Annette was already furious at his interference in her relationship with Josh. And in her present mood, she just might break from the family altogether.

Marsha couldn't go to Kathleen, the second obvious choice for help. She was positive her stepmother would insist that her husband be told what was going on. Which brought her back to the starting point.

She chewed at a fingernail, desperate to find a

solution. There simply wasn't anyone else who could help. Annette wouldn't listen to her or their father. And there just wasn't anybody else.

Josh! His name leaped into her mind with the suddenness of a switched-on light. All of this had started with him. He was ultimately the cause for Annette's actions. He was probably the only person that Annette would listen to, but would he help? Her already tense nerves tied themselves in tighter knots because she knew she would never find out unless she asked him.

A phone call would give her a degree of anonymity. Marsha didn't like the idea of confronting him in person with the news of Annette's latest escapade. It was sure to be an uncomfortable experience, but she knew she had to see him. It was possible she wouldn't be able to convince him over the telephone that the situation was really desperate.

Yet she struggled with the decision a few minutes more before she gathered up her courage to seek him out. With her room key tucked safely in her purse, Marsha switched off the lights and left the room.

She could just imagine what they thought at the hotel desk when she asked where Joshua Lord's suite was. A hundred doubts fluttered in her stomach as she approached his door. There were lights on inside, so at least he was home. She crossed her fingers that no one was with him and knocked at the door.

Within seconds her summons was answered

and the door opened to frame a shirt-sleeved Josh Lord. A slight frown narrowed his dark eyes when he saw her. His features were grimly drawn, minus any polite welcome. There wasn't even a flicker of recognition in his look.

"Yes?" It was a peremptory demand to state her business.

"I'm Marsha Long." She thought she should identify herself first and clutched her purse with nervous fingers. "I'm not sure if you remember me, but I'm . . . Annette's sister."

"I remember you," he stated, but his aloof expression didn't change. No attempt was made to put her at ease.

It was going to be harder than she thought. For a panicky instant, Marsha didn't know where to begin. He didn't look like he'd be willing to help at all.

"I need to . . . talk to you about my sister," she managed finally.

If anything, his expression hardened. "There is nothing I want to discuss about her, Miss Long," he replied in a cold flat voice. "You've wasted your time coming here. Good night."

When he started to close the door, Marsha sprang forward in desperation. "No! Please!" she protested, and pushed a hand against the door to keep it from shutting. "I need your help."

The request made him pause. "My help?" Josh repeated, and his flare of interest gave her a fragment of hope.

"Yes," she said, affirming her request, and nervously brought her hand down to her side. "You see, Annette just left to go out with Craig, one of the waiters here at the hotel," she began.

His interest immediately waned. "She's welcome to go out with anyone she pleases. It has nothing to do with me," he stated.

"Yes, it does," Marsha insisted anxiously. "She's only going out with him to spite you and dad."

"That's her business." Again the door started to close on her.

"No, you don't understand!" she burst out in a rush. "She's going to a motel with him!"

Josh visibly stiffened. The sharpness of his gaze seemed to pierce her. "What did you say?" he demanded.

"She's going to a motel with him." She repeated the sentence in a less assertive tone. "I tried to talk her out of it, but she wouldn't listen to me. She's got this wild idea in her head...that it's better to...do it...with someone she doesn't care about." Marsha blushed furiously as she stammered over the words.

"She decided that, did she?" He seemed to snap out the words as the ridge of his jaw appeared to become lined with steel. "And was it part of her plan to send you over here to tell me about it?"

"No!" She breathed out the denial in a burst of alarm, realizing Josh had seen through all of Annette's plottings and maneuverings.

What if she couldn't convince him that this time the situation was genuine and not manufactured by her sister? It couldn't become a case of the boy crying wolf too many times!

"I swear Annette doesn't know I'm here," she vowed, and automatically raised her hand as if taking a pledge. "Honestly, she doesn't."

"You sound very convincing." But skepticism continued to narrow his gaze. "But you are Annette's sister, aren't you?" It was practically an accusation.

"I admit that sometimes...Annette...arranges for things to happen." She struggled with the confession of her sister's guilt—and her own. "And...sometimes she talks me into helping her out."

"Like with the sweater," Josh guessed.

"Yes," Marsha admitted. Agitation surfaced as she tried to convince him that this time it was different. "I'm trying to help her now, but not because she wants me to. It's because she's my sister and I don't want her to make a terrible mistake." All the apprehension that was twisting her into knots threaded itself into her voice. "She doesn't even like Craig—and she's planning to go to bed with him!"

The corners of his mouth tightened in a kind of angry impatience. "You believe that she means to go through with this?" he demanded.

Marsha sighed brokenly and shook her head in vague confusion. "I don't see how she can. But with Annette—I sometimes think I wouldn't put anything past her.'' She looked at him, her rounded blue eyes filled with anxiety. "After last night, when she broke up with you and had that awful quarrel with dad, she's been...different. I don't know how to explain it,'' she finished lamely. "You're the only one who can stop her. Will you help?''

Josh didn't answer directly. "Do you know which motel they were going to?'' His insistence on more information was its own indication.

"No.'' Marsha shook her head as a quiver of relief went through her. "All she mentioned was Craig had a friend who was a night clerk somewhere on motel row.''

"That's a start,'' he muttered grimly, and turned away from the door, leaving it open.

Marsha hovered on the threshold, unsure if she was supposed to enter or if Josh was coming back. She watched him stride across the living room and stop to pick up the phone. Half turning, he looked to see where she was and motioned her into the suite.

Stepping inside, she closed the door. During the ensuing one-sided conversation, Marsha was able to gather that Josh was talking to one of Craig's co-workers and buddies to find out which motel on the strip employed their friend. Obviously he obtained the information. The minute he hung up he was moving toward the door.

"Are you coming?'' He shot the question at Marsha and she nodded, too intimidated by the angered set of his features to speak. With a barely suppressed violence, Josh yanked the door open. "So help me," he muttered under his breath, "if this is another one of her tricks, I'll wring her damned neck!"

ANNETTE HUGGED THE WALL while Craig unlocked the door to the motel room and pushed it open. Her skin felt chilled and she blamed the cold feeling on the motel's air conditioner and the sleeveless sundress she was wearing. Craig curved an arm around her waist to guide her into the room.

"Hey, this isn't bad." He made the pleased declaration as he looked around. "It's even got a king-size bed."

She had already noticed the way the huge bed dominated the room. It seemed appropriate that it was covered with a scarlet spread. The other requisite furnishings in the room were diminished by its prominence.

The paper sack under Craig's arm rattled noisily as he released her to set it down on a long dresser. He hadn't mentioned what was in the sack, but she had already guessed it contained a bottle of liquor.

Switching on the color television set, he glanced at her. "We'll be able to watch it in bed."

His remark drew her attention to the fact that the screen faced the bed. Craig began changing stations to see what was on. It seemed ridiculous to her to pretend they had come here to watch television.

But she went along with him. "Yes, we can."

Satisfied with whatever was playing on one channel, he moved away from the television and took the bottle out of the sack. "Is whiskey okay?"

"Sure." Annette wandered farther into the room and looked around, but the bed was all she really saw.

"I'll get some ice." Craig picked up the Styrofoam bucket the motel provided to the rooms and paused. "There's a pop machine outside. What kind of mix do you want with your whiskey?"

"Whatever you're having will be fine." She didn't care.

Before leaving the room, he stopped to kiss her. "Don't disappear while I'm gone," he winked.

When the door closed behind him, Annette unconsciously rubbed her hand across her mouth to wipe away the moist trace left by his lips. She walked to the bed and set her purse on the nightstand. Half turning, she sat down and pressed her hands on the mattress as if testing its firmness. There was a numbness, a blankness that kept her from feeling or thinking anything.

A scant few minutes later the key turned in the lock, signaling Craig's return. She studied him as he walked in, abstractly noting again his exceedingly good looks, totally unaffected by them.

"One drink coming right up," he said cheerfully.

Suddenly she didn't know why they were going

through all these motions. Television and drinks; that wasn't why they were there. And she preferred to get the whole thing over with.

"Why don't you fix it later, Craig?" Annette stood up and reached behind her neck to unfasten the halter straps of her sundress. In the back of her mind there was the thought that she'd probably welcome the drink later.

She had no awareness of his startled glance as he set the ice bucket and can of pop beside the whiskey bottle. And she didn't notice the way his avid gaze licked over her when the straps fell loose. She was too busy unzipping the back of her dress.

Almost trancelike, Craig moved toward her, unbuttoning his shirt as he walked and tugging it off. Stepping out of her pink dress, she laid it on a chair back. Under the dress she had worn a strapless bra and a lacy half-slip. Her fingers were on the elastic band of her slip when the touch of Craig's hand on her shoulder made her pause.

She turned her head to look at him, her gray eyes blank of any expression, completely lacking the passion that burned in his. There was no resistance when he took her in his arms and began smothering her lips with kisses. His hands were all over her, touching and feeling.

A jarring feeling of revulsion welled inside her as Annette submitted to his lusting embrace. She had thought she could pretend he was Josh, but she suddenly realized she couldn't. He wasn't

Josh. Annette turned away from his mouth, her hands pushing at him. She needed to think.

Craig misinterpreted her action, not seeing it as opposition to his lovemaking but as a desire to expand on it. He unfastened his pants and started to unzip them, his gaze riveted on the agitated rise and fall of her breasts within the supporting cups of the strapless brassiere.

"You're beautiful, Annette," he declared hoarsely.

It was the wrong thing to say. Those were the very words Josh had used. No matter what she had thought previously, Annette knew she couldn't go through with this. She had been a fool to think she could.

"No." She took a step backward, repulsed by the whole idea.

Craig stopped what he was doing and reached out to catch her hand. "Hey, where are you going?" he laughed, and pulled her back. Immediately Annette started to struggle and Craig fought to hold her, suddenly confused. "What's the matter with you?"

"Let me go!" she demanded angrily.

"What are you talking about?" He roughly attempted to overpower her resistance. "This was your idea, remember?"

CHAPTER TEN

SOMEONE RATTLED THE MOTEL-ROOM DOOR, freezing both of them. As Annette turned her head to look at it, the door burst open with explosive force. The color drained from her face as Josh charged in. His hard features were livid with anger when he saw her in Craig's arms. But she wasn't imprisoned in them for long, because Craig was shocked into letting her go. Josh advanced on them with long purposeful strides.

"How did you know I was here?" Her voice was a thin thread.

An instant later she had her answer when Marsha ventured hesitantly into the room. Her cheeks flamed with the realization her sister had informed Josh of her intentions tonight. Humiliation welled in her throat as Annette realized what Josh must be thinking about her now.

"What's he doing here?" Craig demanded an answer from Annette.

But she wasn't given a chance to explain that she hadn't expected Josh to come. Her wrist was seized to pull her out of Craig's reach. Inadvertently Annette looked into the anger of Josh's eyes.

"I'm taking you back to the hotel." His incensed manner indicated that he wouldn't tolerate any arguments.

"Now wait just a damned minute!" Craig bristled in protest at the way Josh was assuming the right to control whether Annette stayed or left. "She came here with me and she'll leave with me."

"Like hell she will." Josh let go of her wrist and turned on him with a snarl.

"I know what you're probably thinking," Craig retorted. "But she came here of her own free will. I didn't twist her arm."

"She may have come here of her own free will, but she's leaving by *my* will," he stressed with little patience. "And zip your pants up before they fall down!"

Craig turned red and quickly fastened them as Marsha hurried to Annette's side. "Are you all right?" she murmured.

"How could you tell him?" she choked on this awful betrayal by her sister.

A pair of soulful blue eyes looked back at her. "I'm sorry, but I didn't know what else to do," Marsha whispered.

"Marsha, get her purse," Josh ordered, and grabbed the sundress off the chair to shove it into Annette's hands. "Put this on."

He stood between her and Craig, a living wall intent on keeping them apart—as if it were necessary. Annette kept her head lowered to avoid eye contact with her angry rescuer as she slipped the dress on and tied the straps behind her neck. She didn't get any further than reaching for the zipper before his hands turned her around and pushed her fingers out of the way.

"If your father doesn't take the belt to you for this dumb stunt, I will," Josh threatened as he roughly pulled the zipper to the top.

She spun around in shock, her gaze rushing to his. "You aren't going to tell him?" Annette breathed in panic.

"Don't bet on it, sweetheart," he replied grimly.

"But you can't!" she protested.

It was bad enough that she had been so stupid to believe she could go through with it. That shame had been doubled with Josh's appearance on the scene. But if her father were told, too, she would die of mortification. How could Josh even threaten such a thing? His challenging stance revealed he could.

"I can and I will," he stated in no uncertain terms.

"I thought you came charging in to rescue me from a fate worse than death," Annette choked on the accusing words, humiliated into anger. "Instead you've only come to deliver me into my father's hands for punishment. You are despicable, Joshua Lord!"

"You aren't winning any prizes, either, but you're damn well going to get what you deserve," he warned.

"You and whose army are going to take me

there?'' she said, challenging his ability to carry out the threat. She turned to her sister, gathering what pride hadn't been stripped from her. ''Come on, Marsha. We're catching a cab and going back to the hotel.''

The instant her attention was diverted, Josh moved in. He grabbed an arm before she could draw it out of his reach, and twisted it behind her back. The sudden application of force angered her still more. It wasn't fair when he was so much stronger.

''You and Marsha are going back to the hotel with me,'' Josh growled somewhere near the vicinity of her ear.

The pressure he was applying arched her backward, giving her little leverage to kick at him. It was impossible to struggle, but that was his intention. Impotency drove her nearly to tears.

''Here.'' The soft rustle of paper followed Josh's voice. At first Annette thought he was talking to her. ''Tell your friend at the desk this should pay for the broken lock on the door.'' He was speaking to Craig, and the paper sound she'd heard was money.

She was propelled out the door. Once they were in the outer hallway of the motel, Josh untwisted her arm but retained an iron grip on her wrist. She strained and turned her arm, trying to pull free as he dragged her along.

''You let me go, Joshua Lord.'' Her voice was low and trembling, near the breaking point, but he didn't deign to reply.

Behind them, Marsha was half running to keep up. It was becoming apparent that she had defected to the enemy. First Marsha had betrayed what Annette had told her in confidence by going to Josh. Now she was allowing Josh to manhandle her this way without offering a single word of support for Annette's stand against him. Annette was desolated.

His car was parked in the lot. She recognized it as they approached. It was in her mind to break free when Josh released her to get in the car. There wasn't any way she was going to let him march her into her father's presence like some delinquent. But Josh knew the way her mind worked too well.

He motioned for Marsha to climb in the back seat. Without releasing his grip on her wrist, he pushed Annette into the car on the driver's side and made her slide past the wheel to the front passenger seat while climbing in behind her.

The second he let go of her, she fumbled for the door handle. "It's locked," Josh informed her tersely, and turned the key in the ignition to start the engine.

With her escape thwarted, Annette glared at him through the stinging tears in her eyes. The thrusting angles of his profile were uncompromisingly male, showing no softness, no yielding. She had never suspected he could be so ruthless, so uncaring.

"I don't know what I ever saw in you," she declared in a low voice made husky by the awful tightness in her throat.

Tearing his gaze from the street and its traffic, Josh shot her a look. "I don't see any halo above your head."

"You aren't really going to take me to my father. You're just trying to scare me." Annette wanted it desperately to be the case.

"You need more than a good scare." The hardness in his reply was ominous.

She swung her gaze to the front, staring blindly out the windshield. "I hate you." There was an unmistakable tremor in her voice.

"Go right ahead and hate me," Josh invited with cold unconcern. "It isn't going to make any difference."

"I must have been crazy to think I loved you," Annette declared tautly.

"Why don't you just shut up, Annette?" Josh demanded on a harsh note, and shot her a silencing look.

The silence in the car became thick and oppressive. Sitting in the back seat, Marsha felt she was waiting for something to explode. The air was much too volatile. Her glance kept darting from one to the other, but they exchanged not a word or a look.

When they arrived at the hotel, Josh parked the car and climbed out to walk around the car and unlock the passenger door. As Annette stepped out, he clamped a hand on her arm. Again Marsha tagged behind them. She wasn't sure if Josh intended to carry out his threat to deliver Annette to their father. The doubt was erased when he led Annette directly to the suite occupied by her father and Kathleen.

At the door, Josh let go of her arm and hooked a hand around her waist to make sure she stayed by his side. Annette stood rigidly, but her flesh burned at the contact. It was too familiar, too possessive. It reminded her of things that it was better not to recall.

"You have no right to do this," she hissed.

Josh merely looked at her, his dark eyes hard as ironwood. His curled fingers rapped on the door with firm authority. At the sound of someone stirring inside, Annette made an involuntary move to avoid this confrontation with her father, but the arm around her waist tightened. Her body was brought against the male length of his. She felt the involuntary reaction of her senses.

"Who is it?" Her father's voice requested identification before he would open the door.

"It's Josh Lord." He raised his voice slightly. "I have your daughter with me." He failed to mention Marsha, hovering in the background.

The door swung inward and Annette's gaze ricocheted away from any contact with her father's. She had glimpsed his frown of disapproval at the sight of the two of them together. She didn't want to contemplate his reaction when he learned why they were there.

"What is this?" he demanded. "What's going on here?"

"May we come in?" Josh requested tersely, ignoring the questions. "Your daughter has something she'd like to tell you."

With grudging acceptance, her father moved out of the door to silently admit them. Josh pushed her inside. After initially offering a stiff resistance, Annette walked farther into the room on her own accord. Both her father and Kathleen were in their robes.

"There was something you wanted to tell me," her father prompted.

"No." She sat down in a chair and crossed her arms, sending Josh a belligerent look. "I never said that."

"Your father has a right to know where you went tonight, Annette," Josh stated with a narrowed look.

"You went out?" Her father shot her a look of surprise.

She stubbornly refused to answer. There was such a thing as self-incrimination. Josh walked over to her chair and bent down, resting a hand on either armrest and forcing her to meet his look.

"Either you tell him or I will," he warned.

"It's none of his business—or yours!" she flashed, because her only protection was anger.

"All right. If that's the way you want it." Josh straightened and turned to face her father. "Annette visited a motel tonight in the company of one of the waiters from this hotel."

"What?" Her father practically exploded. It took every ounce of her control not to visibly wince. "How do you know this?" he demanded.

"Because Marsha came and told me where Annette had gone," Josh replied evenly.

At the mention of his younger daughter, Jordan Long turned on her with a glowering look. "You knew about this?"

Marsha had been impelled into the suite by curiosity and concern, but she hadn't really expected to be on the receiving end of her father's anger. She hesitantly returned his angry look.

"Yes, I knew," she admitted. "Annette told me."

"Why didn't you come tell me?" There was a whiteness to the line of his jaw.

"Because..." Marsha hedged. "I was afraid you'd lose your temper and...you and Annette would quarrel again. So I went to Josh...to see if he would stop her."

Annette struggled against the sensation of dread as her father turned back to her. She couldn't face the angry disgust in his eyes.

"You have some explaining to do, Annette," he stated harshly. "And you can start right now. Who is this man you were with?"

"His name is Craig," she retorted, and pushed out of the chair, the turmoil inside becoming more than she could contain. "I don't see what all this fuss is about," she bluffed. "Nothing happened!" Her hands sliced the air in emphasis of the assertion.

"You go to a motel room with a man and I'm not supposed to be upset about that?!" her father challenged.

"It's none of your affair what I do!" Annette retaliated, then included everyone in the room. "No one asked any of you to interfere."

Kathleen stepped forward, her hazel eyes soft with concern. "Why did you do it, Annette? Why did you go there with him?"

The gentleness of her stepmother's voice almost proved to be her undoing. It was the first real promise of sympathy she'd received.

She lowered her head in remorse, her voice becoming husky when she answered, "I thought it was what I wanted to do."

"And it turned out that it wasn't," Kathleen guessed.

Annette started to admit it until she caught Josh watching her with his expressionless dark eyes. Her glance fell away from him.

"Josh came before anything happened," she said tightly, and refused to clear herself.

The stubborn streak in Annette wouldn't allow her to confess that she had changed her mind before he arrived. He might interpret it to mean that he was the only one she wanted to make love to her. She didn't want him to know she'd got cold feet at the last minute. She wanted him to feel partially to blame for rejecting her.

"Thank God for that," her father muttered, but he was partially interrupted by a knock at the door. Swearing under his breath, he strode across the room to answer it.

A respite was the last thing Annette wanted. Her legs were shaking and she felt sick. She wanted to crawl off in some corner and die. Returning to the chair, she sank onto its support as her father opened the door.

"Mr. Long?" The male voice that traveled into the suite lifted her head. Her first thought was that it was impossible; it couldn't be Craig.

"Yes," her father replied abruptly.

"I'm Craig Fulton," he identified himself, then went quickly on to why he was there. "I was with your daughter tonight. I knocked on her door to make sure she got back all right, but nobody answered. I wondered if—"

"*You* are the one she was with?" her father demanded.

"Yes, sir," Craig's voice admitted. "Is she here?"

"Yes." It was a terse answer, thick with anger.

"May I come in, sir?" he requested. "I'd like to explain what happened."

"By all means." The agreement was almost a challenge as her father swung the door wide to admit him.

A sinking feeling went through Annette. She had no idea what Craig had to explain. All the facts damned her. She realized that he was obviously intent on clearing himself, probably so he wouldn't lose his job at the hotel. Her glance went to Josh. He was watching her instead of the activity at the door. She looked just as quickly away, fully aware of his low opinion of her.

"Are you all right, Annette?" Craig asked, as if he were concerned about her welfare.

When she looked at him she saw the nervousness beneath his handsome features. Whatever flaws Craig might have, lack of courage wasn't one of them. Except Annette wasn't sure whether he was being brave or stupid coming here like this.

"I'm fine." Her answer was a little clipped. "What are you doing here?" Couldn't he see she was in enough trouble?

"I wanted to be sure you got back okay," he said, repeating the explanation he'd given her father at the door. His glance slid to Josh. The line of his mouth continued to remain grim and his alert gaze missed nothing.

"You were going to explain about tonight, Mr. Fulton," her father reminded Craig of his statement in a challenging tone.

"Yes, sir," Craig reaffirmed, angling his stand to face both Annette and her father. His attitude was very respectful, his posture erect. "I know how it probably must seem, Annette and I alone in a motel room, but we just wanted privacy to talk over some things."

"And you were 'talking' when I came in?" Josh taunted. "That's why Annette was in her slip and you had your shirt off. I suppose you were just getting comfortable."

Annette didn't have to look; she could feel the censorious gray of her father's eyes pillorying her. She felt small, and glared her resentment at Josh for adding another piece of damning information.

"Why are you still here?" she demanded of him, her voice taut and brittle. "Nobody asked you to stay, Joshua Lord, so why don't you just get out of here? This has nothing to do with you."

"Don't compound your problems with rudeness, Annette," her father stated, and swung a grim look at Josh. "You're welcome to stay, Mr. Lord. In fact, I prefer that you do."

"Thank you." Josh inclined his head in quiet deference to her father's authority over this situation. When his dark glance returned to Annette, there was a mocking gleam in it that was glittery and hard.

With that issue settled, her father brought the focus back to Craig. "I believe we left off with you and Annette half-undressed to have your private 'talk.'"

In the face of such evidence, Craig couldn't very well persist in his claim that it had all been innocent. Annette was partially relieved when he didn't try. It would have insulted her father's intelligence and made the situation worse if he had.

"Sir, I admit that I thought Annette might let me make love to her," he confessed. "You have only my word that when Mr. Lord arrived at the motel, Annette had already refused me. I respect your daughter, sir, and I care about her a great deal. That's why I came tonight. And I hope that my being here proves that I'm telling the truth. Annette felt it was wrong."

There was a lessening of tension in the air, as if her father breathed easier, but it didn't last long for Annette. Almost instantly she was under attack from Josh.

"Is that true?" He wasn't taking Craig's word for it. He demanded hers.

"Yes, it's true!" She was goaded into admitting it, and his piercing study stiffly fused her nerves with frissons of guilt.

Craig had returned her reputation to her intact, but she felt the self-punishing need to blacken it in Josh's eyes. A desire to do it before he did.

"What Craig omitted telling you was that I did go to that motel with the intention of going to bed with him," she declared with a defiant tilt of her chin.

"Then why did you change your mind?" Josh challenged smoothly.

Annette didn't want to tell him the answer to that. She averted her head to escape his gaze. "I just did, that's all." She mumbled the reply.

Craig began to speak, bringing the center of attention back to him. "I want you to understand, Mr. Long," he said to her father, "that I'm not interested in just a casual relationship with your daughter. I care about Annette very much."

Impatience and irritation rippled through her. The only person Craig cared about that much was himself, and Annette knew it. It wasn't her name he was interested in clearing as much as it was his.

"Will you stop being so noble, Craig?" she flared. "In another minute you're going to be volunteering to do the *honorable* thing by marrying me."

Craig opened his mouth to respond, but Josh

cut in, "And that can't be, since Annette is going to marry me."

The calm statement jarred Annette to her feet. "What?" She was furious at his supposition she would accept. After all he'd put her through tonight—humiliating her in front of her family—he was crazy to think she'd fall all over herself accepting his proposal. She stood before him, her arms rigidly at her sides and her hands clenched into fists. "I wouldn't marry you if you were the last man on earth!"

Josh wasn't impressed by her anger or her denial. His gaze was coolly indifferent as it ran over her face. "Where you are concerned, I am the last man on earth," he stated simply.

For a long second, her gaze silently battled with his before Annette chose retreat. "I've had enough of this." Her voice trembled its anger through tightly clenched teeth. "I'm getting out of here."

She half turned to march out of the room in high dudgeon, but Josh snared her arm and hauled her back. Struggling, she tried to break loose. Her angry resistance seemed to arouse his own anger.

"You aren't going anywhere," he informed her with tight-lipped grimness. "I can't make up my mind whether you need a husband or a keeper."

"I don't need you!" She hurled the bitter words at him as his fingers dug into the soft flesh of her arms to hold her, inflicting pain.

"It's about time somebody took you off your father's hands," Josh declared roughly. "You've caused him enough grief already." His hard gaze swung away. "With your permission, Mr. Long, I'm taking Annette as my wife."

Turning her head to look at her father, Annette watched the transformation on his face as his look changed from grim paternal outrage to a kind of pleased and mocking satisfaction. She couldn't believe it. He didn't like Josh.

"You have my permission—and my sympathy." A near smile edged the corners of his mouth.

"No!" Annette gasped in shock. "You can't mean it."

But the suggestion of a smile just increased. Her father didn't bother to reply. Instead he turned to Craig. "I believe your presence here has become superfluous, Mr. Fulton." He took him by the arm and guided him to the door. "Thank you for coming."

A little bewildered, Craig let himself be turned out. The door remained opened after he left and her father sent a pointed glance at his younger daughter.

"It's time you called it a night, isn't it, Marsha?" He prompted her departure.

Motionless in the grip of Josh's hands, Annette watched in disbelief as first Craig left, then Marsha. The door was closed and her father walked to Kathleen, curving an arm around her shoulders and turning her in the direction of the adjoining bedroom.

"Where are you going?" Annette demanded. "You can't leave me here with him."

The gray of her father's eyes gleamed with a smile. "I think my future son-in-law can handle the situation without my help."

"I'm not going to marry him," she insisted.

"Yes, you are," Josh stated, attracting her gaze back to him.

His certainty infuriated her. It wasn't right that he should be so sure of her, so positive she would agree. Silver fires blazed in her eyes.

"No, I'm not!" Annette retorted.

Her father's voice intruded on their disagreement in a low murmur. "We'll leave you two to sort it out."

THERE WAS ONLY ONE CHAIR in the darkened room where their son slept. Jordan guided Kathleen to it. "We're going to be in here for a while, so we might as well make ourselves comfortable." He spoke softly, so that he wouldn't disturb the sleeping boy. Taking the chair for himself, he drew Kathleen onto his lap.

"You certainly reversed your opinion of Josh in a hurry," she murmured, and curved a hand around his neck, absently letting her fingers seek the dark tendrils of his hair.

"Until tonight he hadn't proved to me he was the right man for her," Jordan replied.

"Now you're convinced." Kathleen eyed him with warm amusement.

His hand moved along her arm and caressed

the rounded bone of her shoulder in a leisurely fashion. "The next problem will be adjusting to the idea of becoming a grandfather." He smiled.

"I wouldn't worry about it," she murmured. "You'll make a very sexy grandfather."

"That's because I'm married to a sexy grandmother," Jordan assured her, and let his lips find hers in the dark to show just how powerful the attraction was.

ANNETTE STRAINED in Josh's hold, her fingers flattened against his chest. "You're crazy if you think I'm going to marry you." She repeated the denial the instant her father and stepmother left the room. "Just because I thought I loved you—"

"You do love me," Josh interrupted with unwavering sureness.

"I don't!" she snapped.

His mouth crooked. "Do you want me to prove it?" he taunted.

"No, I—" She broke off the denial, saving her energy to resist as his hold on her shifted.

The iron band of his arm circled the back of her waist to force her against his length while he combed his fingers into her tawny hair to hold her head still. Annette tried to elude his descending mouth and failed.

Her lips stayed stiff under the persuasive pressure of his mouth as it coaxed and urged them to respond. It was agony to resist the burning warmth of his kiss. She could feel it melting her limbs and firing her senses. And she suddenly wondered what was the use in fighting it and began kissing him back.

Josh insisted on a total surrender, not content until she was clinging to him and caressing him with trembling hands. Only then did he draw back while she shuddered with the intensity of her longing. His encircling arms continued to support her.

"Say you love me." The disturbed pitch of his voice vibrated over her downcast head. "I want to hear it again."

"I love you, Josh," she admitted reluctantly.

"And you're going to marry me," he said, insisting that she voice her agreement.

A barely audible cry of anguish came from her throat. There were tears in her eyes when she lifted her head to look at his ruggedly handsome face. His velvet gaze seemed to caress her.

"You don't want to marry me, Josh," Annette declared, and reminded him, "You don't even love me."

"Oh, but I do," he corrected with a twinkling gleam in his eyes.

"But—" Her breath became caught in her throat. She couldn't believe that he meant it, not after the things he'd said the other night. "All you wanted was an affair. That's what you told me."

"Yes," Josh admitted, and stroked her cheek and the side of her hair as if he enjoyed touching her. "At the time, I thought that was all I wanted."

"And you don't? You didn't?" She didn't know which it was, past or present tense, or both.

"It took me a while to realize the kind of affair I wanted with you was the permanent kind that comes with marriage," he said to make his meaning clear. "You have your sister to thank for that."

"Marsha?" Annette was too dazed by the wondrous discovery that he loved her when she had thought it was all so hopeless.

"Yes, Marsha." Josh smiled. "When she came to my suite tonight and told me you'd gone to some motel with Craig, I was rudely awakened to the fact that I was in love with you. The thought of any other man having you made me jealous as hell."

"But...you said that men don't marry virgins." How well she remembered those painful words.

"What I meant," Josh said with a curving smile, "was that I don't make love to virgins, then marry them. And that's true, because I'm going to marry you first."

"Josh." His name was an aching little cry of sheer pleasure.

Further discussion of the subject became non-essential as Annette gave herself up to the delights of his embrace, and love circled them in a golden halo.